Westward Dreams

Sarah Lamb

A thank you to my proofreader, Brooke, and all of the lovely women who help ARC read to catch those typos I miss!

This book was not written by AI. Any typos are proudly (and embarrassingly!) my own human created ones!

This book is not allowed to be used in training AI.

Paperback ISBN: 978-1-960418-57-9

Large print ISBN: 978-1-960418-58-6

Contents

May your once upon a time always have a happily ever after, even if there's a dark moment halfway through.

Chapter 1

1880s, Missouri

Mary Clinton tucked the train ticket into her handbag and took a last look around the small room she'd called hers for the last three years. Little flutters of excitement filled her from the top of her head to the soles of her button-up boots. It felt almost surreal to be leaving everything behind—not that there was much.

A small bed, a washstand, a row of pegs to hang her dresses, and a wooden chair had been her furnishings. There hadn't been a window in her tiny room, and that had always made her a little sad. Mary enjoyed seeing the sky so full of clouds or stars. In her new home, she'd want windows everywhere, with gauzy curtains to let the light in. She'd been saving up so that one day, they could even have panes of glass in them.

"Do I have it all?" she asked herself, stooping to check under the bed once more. She doubted there was anything there, as she'd already swept the room twice over, but it was better to check once more than to have that niggling feeling of wonder her entire journey.

Once she'd determined nothing of hers remained, Mary stood and squared her shoulders. "Right then."

It was time to leave. Cal—and her new life—were waiting for her in Oregon. The train would get her much of the way there, and she'd seek a stage or a hired wagon for the rest. Mary had never traveled so far before and was a little anxious about doing it on her own. For days, she'd been hoping she wouldn't get on the wrong train or have a pickpocket sit next to her.

She'd gone so far as to sew most of her money into her dress in a secret pocket. She'd left enough out for expenses, of course, but Mary had almost *three hundred dollars*. In addition to working so hard for the Miles family, she spent her evenings on what Cal had called a fit of fancy, sewing matching little girl and doll dresses. Mary had thought she'd like to open a shop one day selling her creations, but then she'd met Cal, and he told her there was no need; he'd care for her fully.

Still, it was good to have something to fall back on, just in case. While she was sure she wouldn't need such a thing, Mary was glad to have her skill with a needle, and the extra money that had brought in. She did wish she could bring just a little more of her sewing supplies with her. However, it would have been difficult to carry anything beyond her two carpet bags on such a journey alone, so she'd given it away to others.

Actually, she'd given away most of her belongings. She wouldn't lie; it made her feel unprepared. It wasn't a feeling she liked, but Mary was determined to make the best of her situation, even if she'd be starting over.

How much nicer it would have been to bring the things she wanted to start her new soon-to-be-wedded life out West, but Cal told her he would get whatever they needed. Though Mary had her doubts on that, a man surely wouldn't think of everything that was needed, especially the things a woman would want, what choice did she have but to agree?

Cal had kissed her goodbye and left over a year prior to claim land under the Homestead Act. He was there now with a hundred acres part of the way to being his. His last letter had spoken of a small two-room house he was building, and how he couldn't wait to see her again. He promised a larger house in the future, adding on a room a year until she was satisfied, and Mary couldn't help but dream about what that might look like.

She longed to have a home with several bedrooms, a large kitchen, a comfortable sitting room, and of course, windows! Windows everywhere, so she could see the beautiful mountains she'd heard about, the wide-open spaces, and the flowers she'd be planting.

But that could wait. First, she had to arrive. Mary was anxious to get there, and excited to see Cal again. She'd wanted to go with him to claim the land, but he'd told her to stay. They'd get married later. That had confused her, as surely it would have been easier to travel together with their belongings. Why, she could have even made dresses on the way to sell once there, but Cal was insistent.

As he knew more about such things since two of his friends had gone the year before, and Cal told her how important it was for him to get a home built before she came, Mary had reluctantly agreed to the wait. What was her alternative? Cal was a handsome man, and a hard worker. He could easily have his pick of any woman around. That he chose her still filled her with wonder and surprise.

And Mary was not about to jeopardize it.

She'd waved goodbye the morning he left in a wagon train, watching a little enviously as other couples marched away excitedly. A passing reverend had offered to marry them the night before. Mary had eagerly looked at Cal, but he'd shaken his head no. It crushed her, but he'd asked her to wait and that's what she'd do. It was true it would be much nicer arriving and moving into a house right away than staying in their wagon or under a tent until one was built, so she tried to find courage in the fact he cared for her comfort.

Mary continued working as housemaid for the Miles family, saving her pay to give to Cal when she arrived. They'd no doubt need it for their homestead. Mary wasn't quite sure what all was involved with creating one, but she was more than willing to do her part to make their shared dream come true. In her last letter, she told him how much she'd managed to save, and was sure he'd be thrilled.

As the time grew closer for her to leave, with a little sadness, Mary had sold or given away everything she couldn't squeeze into her bags. She'd packed and repacked, trying to fit all she could in the bags, but far more had to stay than go with her.

It had been hardest to say goodbye to her books, and she hoped she'd be able to replace them. Cal hadn't ever understood that she enjoyed reading, so Mary suspected they wouldn't be very high on his priority list of things to buy.

Her extra pair of boots and her clothing was much more important to bring, she knew, even if she wished it wasn't so. Hopefully the money she'd gotten would help her replace the volumes one day, and the blankets she'd once carefully made in what little free time she had, thinking they'd adorn her future home.

There was a knock on her door, pulling her from her thoughts. Mary called out, "Come in!"

Martha, who was the Miles' family's housekeeper, walked in. "All packed?" she asked.

"I am." Mary glanced around once more. "It's strange to think I'm leaving this afternoon."

"I will miss you," Martha said. "You were quiet and always worked hard. Not many like you. Be sure to write and tell me how you are."

As Mary nodded, she said, "Thank you for all you've done for me. You've treated me so kindly, and taught me so much."

"Enough of that," Martha sniffed. "You'll make me cry. Best get going now, or you'll miss your train. But, oh!" The woman offered an envelope. "From Mrs. Miles, with thanks. It's your last wages."

Sniffling herself as she accepted it, Mary picked up her bags and left her room. Her last wages. The time had come. She was really leaving.

Slowly, she walked down the small hallway one last time, and through a back door. Once outside, Mary paused on the rocky path and glanced back at the large home behind her.

The Miles family had been good to work for; they'd been fair and kind. It had been what she'd needed at the time. But now, she was going to have a home of her own. It was something she was ready for. After all, she was twenty-six now. It was past time to make her own way, and build her own future.

That thought erased the tears, and Mary squared her shoulders. Her heart felt light, even though her bags were quite heavy as she hurried toward the train station. She could hear the whistle in the distance, and hoped she'd make it in time. The train would only stop for a few minutes before it departed again. If she missed it, there wouldn't be another for days.

Slightly panting, Mary made it to the station as the train pulled in, its brakes screeching loudly. Brushing the soft brown strands of hair from her face, she offered her ticket to the conductor, who pointed her to her car.

Mary found a seat and set her bags down next to her. Her arms ached from carrying them, and though she missed her books already, she knew she'd made the right choice. They were simply too heavy to bring. The other housemaids would enjoy them, though.

Curiously, Mary glanced around her. The train wasn't full, and so it appeared she wouldn't have to share a row with anyone. She was glad of that. A little more space for herself, and some quiet for her thoughts. As she'd never been on a train before, she wanted to enjoy her trip, and that would best be done without another next to her.

Her fingers itched to keep busy, as was her habit, but as she had no needle, thread, nor fabric, and no books at all, she'd simply have to content herself with the view and her thoughts.

The train's whistle sounded again, filling her ears with its rich tone and her body with excitement. This was it! Slowly, the train lurched forward, and Mary watched out the windows as all of her memories of the town flooded her at once.

She had no one waving at her as she pulled away from the station, but she didn't need that. This was her past.

Half-day-off shopping trips with the other housemaids, warm summer picnics, and how she'd met Cal at one of them. It had been such a surprise that first day when he'd said hello. And how, after a year, he'd asked her out.

Mary rested her head against the glass window and smiled. She'd been the envy of the other housemaids. Not that she'd let Cal distract her from her work. Never! But soon, she'd be spending her days working side by side with him, and if he distracted her then...well, there was no harm in that!

A few seats in front of her, a happy couple sat, leaning in closely and talking, with smiles on their faces. In just days, that would be her. After more than a year apart, there'd be so much to talk about. Letters couldn't be filled with as much as she wanted to say. There were so many things she felt, but had no words to express.

The train picked up speed, and the green pasture alongside her started to blur. How much would the scenery change on the way? She didn't know, but was eager to find out.

"Just a few more days," Mary whispered as she looked up at the bright blue sky, her eyes following a hawk's path. "Then all my westward dreams come true."

Chapter 2

"Why must you go, Papa?"

Simon Alexander latched his suitcase and set it reluctantly next to the smaller bag he'd already packed. His eyes met those of his serious-faced daughter.

"Because, I must. It is my job. You know I am the manager of several banks, and I must travel time to time to check on them."

"But I shall miss you." Julia's lip wobbled. "You aren't usually gone for so long."

It was true. This would be the longest he'd ever been away from her, nearly two months. The very thought of it made him feel apprehensive. Not for the train, no. He enjoyed the swaying and the scenery and the towns he'd stop at. The train would take him in a large loop, and he wouldn't stay more than a few nights each at nearly a dozen locations, as he went over ledgers and talked to bank employees. Nothing difficult.

What unsettled him was leaving Julia behind. It was clear she felt the same. Could he blame her? They were all the family the other had.

"I could pack quickly," she said hopefully. "We could go there together."

"We've talked about this," Simon said. "This is a business trip. I can't bring you. You'd have nothing to do, and," he added, holding up a hand to stop her protests, "it's not safe to leave you alone, nor proper for me to bring you there."

Her shoulders drooped as she nodded. "Yes, Papa."

Though he knew she didn't fully understand, being here at their large home with a beautiful yard and garden, and with the wonderful housekeeper he'd found in Mrs. Thomas shortly after Julia's birth, would be much better for her. Even if he'd miss her with all his being.

"I will tell you what," Simon said. "I will give Mrs. Thomas permission to take you into town once a week while I'm gone. You may choose a small treat for yourself as well, perhaps a candy stick or a new hair ribbon? I will let you have a dime for each outing."

That made Julia's face light up, and she scurried from the room, no doubt to find the housekeeper and tell her the news. Usually, those rare treats were only allowed a few pennies.

Simon crossed the room for his hat and glanced down at a picture Julia had drawn him the evening before. It was of the two of them, her on her swing, and a smile on her face.

It was Simon's goal to always keep it there. Keeping Julia safe and content was of his utmost concern, and he couldn't do that if she wasn't close to home. She was a quiet girl, shy, sweet, and sheltered, and he intended to keep her that way. All too soon, her eight years of age would turn into eighteen, and she might want to leave home for her own life.

Time had a way of speeding up when one didn't expect it to. Simon stopped and studied his face in the mirror. Were those a few silver hairs? He was thirty-four now, and had been through a good deal of stress and worry since his beautiful wife had passed away. Life had changed in an instant, and had never been the same again. It was a wonder he didn't have wrinkles as well.

He shook his head, pushing all memories of Meghan to the very corners of his heart, where he kept them safely locked so he wouldn't lose anything of her. He couldn't bear if he forgot, and it had gotten so much harder to recall her sweet voice, her laughter that had tinkled. The smell of her perfume.

He had to keep those memories safe. Keeping them buried deeply within him was the only way to protect them. It was also better that way, because then there was less pain. No tears or sorrow if some were to escape. He'd had enough of both, as he'd held her one last time and then again as she'd been laid to rest.

He owed their daughter his strength. How else would she learn that tragedies and adversity could be overcome? Even if he wasn't completely sure it could, he needed to try to be an example for her.

Simon stepped away from the mirror. It was time to go. He didn't want to miss the stagecoach that would take him to the train. With a last check for his ticket, Simon picked up his bags and walked down the long hallway to the stairs of his two-story home, his footsteps echoing in the emptiness.

He and Meghan had planned to fill the many bedrooms with children. Instead, fate took her too soon, and two of the rooms sat empty, the others occupied by himself, Julia, and Mrs. Thomas.

In addition to those rooms, there was a large dining room, his study, a sitting room, a library, the kitchen, and a day room, where Julia often did her schooling or played with her dolls. And, there was the attic.

"Are you leaving now, Papa?" Julia's soft voice came from the sitting room, and he set his bags down so he could tell her goodbye properly.

"I am, my dear," he told her, walking in to join her for a moment. "Mrs. Thomas will be taking very good care of you, and I'll be back before you know it."

"Indeed, I will," the older woman said, from where she'd been sitting in a corner chair mending something. "Julia has told us we will be taking outings into town weekly. But, have you put any thought into my suggestion?"

He frowned. "I apologize. What suggestion was that?"

"A governess," the housekeeper said, a little exasperated. "Someone to both be a companion and a teacher for our young miss."

"Ah. That's right."

He had put thought into it. And promptly dismissed the idea a few seconds later, which was why he had forgotten. There would be no one who could care for his daughter the way he could. As for a companion, Julia hadn't ever complained of being lonely. She had plenty of books and dolls, and he oversaw her education himself. In fact, for the last week he'd been writing out her lessons to do while he was gone.

To his surprise, however, as he started to reply to Mrs. Thomas, he saw Julia's eager face. Something made him stop, and ask, "Is that...something you'd like?"

"Yes, Papa," Julia answered quickly. "Might I have a governess? It would be so much easier to learn from one. And so nice to have her play with me. We could go for walks, and she could teach me all kinds of things. Mrs. Thomas gets busy running the house. It would ease her burdens as well."

Simon hesitated. Her reasoning was logical, and he couldn't outright refuse her, not when he'd be leaving. Her sad face wasn't something he wanted to see as his final memory of her this trip, and he didn't want her pouting or disappointed, making their separation more difficult for her.

So, he sighed and said, "Well, I will think on it. Now," he stood from where he'd been sitting next to Julia on the sofa, "you be good and I will see you soon."

Julia wrapped her arms around his middle, and he held her tightly before stepping back. "If I can, I will bring you a surprise," he promised.

Her face lit up at the words, and she nodded.

"Mrs. Thomas, you have the hotels I'll be at and the dates," Simon said. "So, if you need me you can send a message. Please, though, only if it's urgent."

The housekeeper nodded, and Simon picked up his bags and left, heading toward the town. It wasn't too much of a walk, and he'd rather stretch his legs while he could, than go to the bother of hiring a wagon.

He glanced over his shoulder once and waved to Julia and Mrs. Thomas, then faced forward again.

A governess. He knew the two of them wanted him to hire one. But it wouldn't happen. As he'd told himself for the last eight years, there was no one who could care for Julia the way he did. Why even bother to try and then disappoint the child or himself?

When the time came that the woman would leave, be it years or only months that she stayed, it would hurt his daughter. She'd already had one person leave her life. She didn't need to experience the pain of another loss.

It was better to keep one's heart locked up forever. Opening it would only lead to sorrow.

Chapter 3

The stage came to a stop, and Mary joined the passengers scrambling out of it. Her lungs ached for clean air, not the overpowering smell of passengers who hadn't been able to wash for days.

For nearly four hours, she'd sat next to a man who had the most horrible wet cough. She felt quite ill, and prayed it was simply the dust aggravating his lungs, not some sort of sickness coursing through him that would cause her to become unwell. The other passengers must have had the same thought, for they each scrambled away from the man, who was acting quite unbothered by their response to his repeated coughing.

Their bags were unloaded, and Mary quickly took possession of hers. She then stood, glancing around for

Cal. Where was he? She'd written and told him what day she'd arrive. Perhaps he just hadn't gotten there yet.

A vacant bench wasn't too far away, and she walked to it and sat. Time passed very slowly as she looked around. From her vantage point, she couldn't see much of the town, just a small fragment, as it was blocked by the stagecoach office.

She waited for so long, the other passengers left. Mary was starting to feel nervous. Finally, after perhaps an hour, she walked to the stage office. There, a schedule was posted. It looked as though another stage would be arriving and departing that day. Did Cal think she was on that one? She really didn't want to wait. Perhaps if he had come to town to seek her, she could go to their homestead herself and be there waiting as a surprise!

"Help you, Miss?" the man asked, patiently looking at her as she studied the schedule.

"I could use it," Mary admitted. "I thought my intended was going to meet me, but perhaps my letter didn't arrive to him letting him know which day I was going to be here. Do you know where I might find the plot of land Cal Lynch owns?"

"That I don't," the man told her, "but you see that building over there with the green door? That's the land office. They should be able to help you out easily."

"Thank you," Mary said, picking up her bags and walking toward the indicated building. A man was coming out as she approached, and held the door for her. She thanked him, and walked in, glancing around.

The building wasn't too large, but it was filled with charts and maps on the walls, several books lined neatly on a shelf and a desk, where a tall man wearing glasses sat on a wooden chair.

"Excuse me," Mary said timidly. "I'm looking for Cal Lynch's land. He's my intended, and I am trying to find him."

"Lynch," the man muttered. "Let me see here, Miss." He pulled a book toward him, and flipped through the pages, eventually running his finger down a column. Once he'd found what he was looking for, he went to one of the maps on the wall, and pointed. "Right here."

Mary stared where he pointed. It meant nothing to her. "How will...how will I find it?" she asked.

"Well, there's a man usually in front of the general store willing to drive folks in his wagon for pay," the man offered. "Want me to check?"

"If you'd be so kind," Mary said. "I would be grateful."

"Be right back," the man said.

As he left, she studied the map on the wall, and let her finger touch the spot the land office manager had. Their land. What did it look like? Was it green? Filled with rocks or trees? In just a short time, her questions would be answered, but best of all, she'd be back again with Cal, and she could hardly wait.

This was the day her dreams came true. How soon would they marry, she wondered? Today, surely, so she could sleep at their new home. She wondered where the church was. How would they get back into town to find it? Did Cal have a wagon or just a horse?

The sound of a wagon pulling up brought her attention back to where she was, and Mary stepped outside. The man from the land office gave her a smile. "Jim here will drive you, Miss, for a dollar."

"Thank you," Mary said, directing the words to each man.

Jim put her bags in the back of the wagon and helped her up. He shook the reins, and they swiftly started to leave town.

"First time in Oregon?" he asked her.

"Yes. It's beautiful," Mary told him. "I am amazed the mountains in the distance still have snow, though it's summer."

"Pretty, aren't they?" Jim said. "We have some majestic scenery around here."

"I can see that," Mary told him. "I appreciate you driving me."

"Not any trouble at all," the man assured her. "We aren't too far. Be there before you know it."

Mary tried not to fidget or seem impatient, but she was excited to see Cal again. She was sure his face would be one of surprise, and then joy when they caught glimpse of each other.

"Just that way, around this curve," Jim said suddenly.

Sitting up expectantly, Mary stared all around her, wanting to memorize her new home. As soon as they went around the curve, she could see a small house on the horizon. "That must be it!" she gasped, sitting up as tall as she could to see more, one hand shading her eyes from the sun.

"Sure is," the man said. "That's the Lynch claim."

"I wonder where Cal is," Mary murmured.

The wagon came to a stop, and she climbed down, glancing about. "Hello?" she called. "Cal?"

She was about to call again, when the house door opened, and two surprised faces stared at her. One was Cal, the other a woman whose arms were around him.

Mary felt the breath leave her body, and lightheadedness swept over her. She wasn't sure just what was going on, but instinct told her it wasn't good.

"Who's that?" the woman asked.

Cal stepped closer. "Mary? Is that you?"

"Yes," Mary whispered, pressing her hands into her stomach to stop their trembling. "Who...who is she?"

"I'm Mrs. Lynch," the woman said. She giggled then. "Or, soon to be."

"I can explain," Cal said, coming closer.

Mary stepped backward, and her back struck the side of the wagon. She was acutely aware of Jim watching, and was glad he hadn't returned to town. She knew she'd be going back with him. How could she stay? Cal had replaced her.

Slowly, she shook her head in disbelief. "I waited for you," Mary said, her voice wobbling. "Worked hard and long days as a housemaid, and saved for our future. All that time you were...what?"

"With me," the other woman said, shrugging. "I reckon he got tired of waiting."

"Now, honey," Cal started, taking a step toward her.

"Don't honey me," Mary said, lifting her chin. "Unless...were you talking to her?"

"Look," Cal said, not even having the decency to look embarrassed. "I'm sorry. Don't know quite what happened. I got here, was building the house, and met Doris. And she and I...well..."

"I'm expecting," Doris said loudly.

Mary wasn't sure if the loud gasp came from her or from Jim, but she steeled herself, pushing every one of the hurt emotions into a tiny corner of her heart and locking them away. "I see," she finally said. "Congratulations." She turned then. "Sir, would you drive me back to town?"

"Right away," Jim promised.

"Now wait a minute!" Cal shouted. "What about that money you were bringing me?"

Teeth clamped so tight her jaw ached, Mary clambered over to the wagon. How dare he ask about that? Mary climbed in the wagon, and refused to look back over her shoulder. She was tense with anger, but worse than that, a terrible pain she'd never known before.

Cal's shouts for her to wait came, but were soon covered by the sound of the wagon creaking away. Mary had always thought it dramatic in books when the heroine talked about her world crashing down upon her, and an empty void within their soul. But...that's just how she felt right now.

It was hard to catch her breath, and her eyes burned with unshed tears. It didn't matter. Mary focused as hard as she could as she faced forward. She wouldn't let Cal see the tears tracking down her cheeks.

"He don't deserve those," Jim said quietly, offering her a handkerchief as his wagon rattled back to town and her tears finally fell.

"I'm not sure what I should do now," Mary said quietly. "I feel like a fool."

"Only fool is him, passing up a good woman like you for a floozy," Jim said. "I know Doris. She won't be around long. Moves from one to the next."

Mary dabbed her eyes. "She can keep him. I won't go back there." She took a deep breath and slowly let it out. "Do you know of anyone hiring? I'm not keen on staying in the same town as Cal, but until I figure out what I want to do, I've no choice."

"Let me think." Jim rubbed at his jaw. "There's some businesses in the town. Did I hear you say you were a housemaid? There are a few large houses just on the edge of town. Might be one of them wants somebody."

"Thank you," Mary said. "Do you also have a dressmaker in town? I've skill with a needle. Perhaps one needs help."

"No, ma'am," he told her. "Most women do it themselves."

"Then I'll start with asking the homes if they need help," Mary said, trying to take comfort in the smallest part of a plan. If one needed a housemaid, or even another pair of hands in the kitchen, that would also provide a roof over her head, something that otherwise she might not have tonight.

She fixed her gaze ahead, her shoulders square. It wasn't ideal, and this wasn't what she'd imagined when she came to Oregon, but this was the situation, and she'd have to make the best of it.

There was simply no other choice.

Chapter 4

Simon's shoulder hit someone. "I'm sorry," the woman said apologetically, as she stepped to the side, keeping her face down. "I wasn't watching where I was going."

"Not a problem," Simon said. "Neither was I."

The woman continued on her way, and he stopped to glance at her once more. Had she been crying? He hesitated, wondering if she needed help. Was there time for him to offer assistance?

"Stage boarding!" the stagecoach manager called.

"Coming! Hold the stage!" Simon bellowed, and jogged the two dozen paces to the loading area. He handed over his bags and then climbed into the stagecoach, managing to secure a spot by the window. The stage wasn't too full this afternoon, carrying only five passengers, including himself.

As the stagecoach shuddered and started, he found himself looking for the young woman he'd nearly collided with. He'd never seen her before, and she was carrying two carpetbags. Did that mean she was new to the area?

It must be hard to travel as a woman alone, if that's what she'd done. Travel itself was a difficult thing, and another reason why he'd not wanted Julia to come. Though children often saw things as adventures and enjoyable—at first—that quickly faded as boredom or discomfort settled in.

Besides, she couldn't be within his sights at all times if they did travel, and he had to keep her safe. Perhaps...perhaps he should consider the idea of a governess. Then, she could travel with him and have a caregiver.

But the idea still bothered him. Home was safe. Travel had risks. It was easy to get lost or hurt, and if something happened to Julia...nothing scared him more. She was all that he had left.

As he'd held Meghan's hand, he'd whispered promises. How much he loved her. That he'd never forget her. Would always, always protect their daughter. He'd vowed nothing would harm Julia, and he would do all in his power to see that to fruition.

Simon took a deep breath and focused on the scenery—distant mountains, a few deer running through a field—instead of his past. Once more, he pushed those feelings away into the corners of his heart, determined to lock them away even tighter. Why had they been escaping so much as of late?

It was mid afternoon, and once they reached the train station, it would be nearing sundown. He reached for the book in his pocket, intending to distract himself. Keeping his mind busy was a sure way not to think about the governess problem.

"Traveling again, Simon?"

He glanced up to see his friend, Jeff Marlin seated across from him. "I didn't even see you! Yes, I am. What about you?"

"Heading to California to check on one of my hotels," Jeff answered. "You know how it is. Got to make the rounds."

"Doing the loop myself," Simon said with a nod.

"Must be hard leaving your daughter for so long." Jeff shook his head. "Glad mine are all grown now. A little different than it would have been back when I was your age."

"Yes, it is hard." Simon frowned. "It's especially difficult this time, because both she and the housekeeper were after me before I left for something."

"Ah," Jeff said with an understanding grin. "Sweets? A doll? Some fancy teas for the housekeeper?"

"Don't I wish it were that simple!" Simon said, shaking his head. "Trifles I can do. No, they wished me to hire a governess."

"Why don't you?" his friend asked. "Our girls had one. Isn't fair to the housekeeper to try and do it all. So she was fond of reminding us, when we first broached the subject."

"We don't need one," Simon said dismissively.

"You don't? Or Julia doesn't?" Jeff asked.

Simon scowled. "None of us do. Shouldn't you be on my side of the situation?"

His friend shrugged. "Your choice. I'm just saying, there's worse things out there your girl could want."

"That's the truth," Simon agreed. Julia did ask for very little. She was generally very content. However, he wished he'd never brought up the subject because now his mind had returned to the question, and the pleading expression Julia had worn.

"How's the business going? Did you get that issue solved with your supplier?" Simon asked, trying to change the conversation's subject.

"Sure did," Jeff said. "Let me tell you just what happened. What a mess it was."

Simon nodded, and let himself be distracted by his friend's recent difficulties in having his newest hotel built. He ignored the older woman across from him reading a newspaper, and the ad he could see that read: *Wanted, governess.* He ignored the book that a young woman was reading, titled: *The Proper Education of Young Ladies,* and he most assuredly did little more than grunt when Jeff brought around the conversation to his oldest daughter, who had just hired a nanny—her old governess.

As the sun started to dip, and the train station was only moments ahead, Simon readied himself to leave the stage, and Jeff.

Hopefully, once he boarded the train, there would be no children, no young women minding children, and nothing at all to remind him of Julia and her request.

It wasn't that it was a bad request. It certainly wasn't an extravagant one. It was just simply, completely, and positively out of the question.

He'd bring Julia a doll or a new book. Mrs. Thomas a tin of sweets. Something small to let them know he'd been thinking of them. He always had. But it wouldn't be a governess.

Simon had no intention of inviting a stranger into his home, let alone letting her get close to his child. There was no way that would happen—ever. Julia would just have to understand. He was doing it for her own good.

Chapter 5

After her near run-in with the handsome man coming in the other direction, Mary realized she needed to pay more attention to her surroundings. What if the man had been irritated with her instead of apologetic? She didn't need anything more happening today to cause a problem. The day had already taken a horrible shift from what she'd originally imagined.

Angry tears sprang to her eyes, but Mary blinked them away. Jim was right. Cal didn't deserve them. Her chest squeezed, and she wondered if she'd ever be able to breathe again without that tightness that crushed her each time she thought about him.

Had she missed a sign that he didn't care for her the way she'd thought? Mary wasn't sure. All she knew was this was the most painful thing she'd ever felt, and she couldn't imagine how her heart would ever heal.

It was better to not think about it. That would be the only way she could survive. She was sure.

Mary suddenly realized she was nearing the edge of the town and paused. In the distance, she could see six large homes. They were quite spaced out, and it would be a long, hot walk to each. She was already tired and thirsty. It was important to think carefully about this. Which might be the most likely to hire her if she asked for a position? Even if it was just short term.

Mary studied each home carefully, hoping that her natural instincts would give her a little nudge toward one.

Nothing.

She sighed heavily. "Fine. Not a thing is going to be easy today, is it?"

Deciding to go to the house on her far left, Mary started to walk on when she heard a sniffle, and then a sob. Surprised, she turned and spotted a little girl curled into a ball against the side of a thick tree. It was so large, it completely hid the child, which was why she hadn't even seen her.

"Are you okay?" Mary asked, coming closer. "Are you hurt?"

The girl looked up at her, and Mary saw her sweet face was red and blotchy. She must have been crying for a while.

"I'm lost," she hiccupped. "I was chasing after Papa, but he was so fast I couldn't catch up. Then I lost him."

"Oh dear!" Mary said, as she looked around, hoping to spot the girl's father, even though she wouldn't know him upon sight. "I can help you look, but perhaps we'd best see if anyone around here has seen him. I've only just arrived to town, and I don't know anyone."

"He's gone now," the girl sniffled. "I saw the stagecoach leave."

"Oh, was your father traveling?" Mary asked. "Is that why you are crying? You miss him?"

"I'm used to him leaving," the girl said sadly. "Mrs. Thomas looks after me while he's gone. But that's not why I'm crying." She wiped at her eyes. "I've gotten all mixed up and don't know where I need to go to get home."

"I see," Mary said. "Well, let's see what we can do about that. Oh! I've not introduced myself. I'm Mary."

"I'm Julia," the girl said, standing as she wiped her eyes once more.

"Where do you live, Julia?" Mary asked.

"In a big green house."

"What is it near?" Mary asked, turning this way and that, hoping to see a green home.

"Nothing," she answered. "Not really. We have a large garden and a swing, and it's somewhere near here, but it's not by anything."

That wasn't very helpful, especially for a stranger such as herself. "I see," Mary finally said. "Well, there's no help for it, we'll need to see if we can find someone who knows where your house is. Shall we try that store there?" she asked.

"Oh no!" Julia said. "I'm not supposed to be here by myself. I will get in terrible trouble with Mrs. Thomas."

"You already are in a bit of trouble," Mary tried to reason. "You're lost. We need to return you before Mrs. Thomas gets worried."

A man walked near just then and paused. "Well, hello, Julia. Out for a stroll? Who's this then?"

Julia ran up to the man. "Mr. Steves! This is Mary." The girl turned to her, and then back to the man, proudly saying, "She's just come to be my new governess."

"Well now, that's just fine," the man said, as Mary's eyes opened wide and her mouth fell open at Julia's words. She was about to correct her when Julia's not very subtle wink stopped her. Perhaps the girl was trying to spare herself the trouble she might get into. Mary understood, and simply nodded.

"Mr. Steves, wait!" Julia said, as the man started to leave. "Mary's bags are heavy and I have gotten us lost. Which way is home?"

The man rubbed at his jaw. "I think if you just walk along this road here, and turn at the blue house, you'll get to yours right quickly. But do you need help with your bags?"

"No, no, I'll be just fine," Mary assured him. "We should be going."

"If you say so," the man agreed.

"Thank you!" Julia said, as Mr. Steves walked away.

It was then Mary took a deep breath and hoped she didn't sound too stern. "Julia, you shouldn't have lied. I'm not your governess."

"Papa said he would think about one," Julia said, with a small shrug of her tiny shoulders. "Mrs. Thomas and I want one very much. Are you here for something else? If not, you could be mine."

Mary opened her mouth and then closed it. How did one explain to a child that they'd come to marry, only to find their intended in the arms of another woman? She couldn't. It wouldn't be appropriate at all. But what could she say that the child might understand, and prevent her from asking further questions?

She hesitated, then finally said, "I find my circumstances have changed from what I expected them to be. I am looking for a job, until I figure out what to do."

"That's perfect," Julia said. "Papa will be gone for quite some time. You can stay with us. You can have the job of being my governess."

"I'm not sure that's a good idea," Mary said. "I'm a stranger. You shouldn't invite strangers into your home."

Julia studied her face for a moment. "You're right," she finally said. "But you won't be a stranger long. I think you and I will be friends. I already like you."

The little girl set off down the road, and Mary scrambled to follow her. She didn't intend to stay, but she did need to make sure the child got home safely. She felt a sense of responsibility toward her.

It wasn't long before they found Julia's home. It was a large house, indeed. Mary wondered how many servants they had, and if they could use another. It wouldn't hurt to ask, since she was here. Perhaps she'd be fortunate to get a job.

"Mrs. Thomas!" Julia called as they entered. "Look! Look!"

"My word, child. You know better than to shout," a woman scolded as she walked into the foyer where Mary stood, looking around. Her eyebrows raised as she spotted her. "Who's this?"

"My governess," Julia said proudly.

"But I thought your papa..." Mrs. Thomas stopped then, as a smile crossed her face. "That man! What a fine trick he played on us. Welcome, welcome! We've been wanting you for a long time. I'm Mrs. Thomas, the housekeeper."

"M-Mary Clinton," she stammered. Mary's eyes went to Julia, and the girl just beamed at her.

"Let's get you settled in," Mrs. Thomas said. "I'll show you to a room."

Mary started to follow her, but Julia's small hand on hers stopped her. "Don't worry," Julia whispered. "I promise it will be okay. You can leave when Papa comes home if you want. I'll tell him it was my idea."

Mrs. Thomas paused, and turned, facing her and Julia. Her eyes went to the little girl. "Just what was your idea?"

The little girl's shoulders sagged, and Mary felt badly, but she knew she had to tell the woman. She wasn't one for lying, and this was far too serious to not speak up.

She took a deep breath, and said, "You see, I came here..." she didn't miss Julia's pleading expression and swallowed, "I came here to seek employment. As a housemaid or a governess. I don't have approval yet from Julia's father. I'm afraid this sweet girl is just a little excited."

"You came here to seek employment?" The housekeeper looked doubtful. "No one just comes here for that. The town isn't large enough."

"She said her circumstances changed," Julia said, almost proudly. "That's why she can be my governess!"

Mary nodded slowly. Her cheeks turned red, and she softly said, "Yes. They have. I came thinking I...I was to marry. But he...he didn't wait."

Mrs. Thomas gave her a sympathetic look. "Oh, my dear. How terrible. I'm so sorry."

"So can she be my governess?" Julia asked.

"Your papa has the final say," the housekeeper said. "But I'd like you to stay. Julia would like you to stay, and Mr. Alexander isn't here for a time. Why don't we call this a trial period? When he gets back, if this has been a success, perhaps he'll let you stay on? If it's not, no harm done. I can't pay you, but I can feed you and house you. Perhaps you'll also be able to figure out an alternative plan, since your original one didn't work out."

"Please, Mary?" Julia asked, wrapping her arms around her waist.

"I'd be grateful for the opportunity," Mary answered. "I've references. I can also sew and cook. I'm used to hard work."

"Then it's settled," Mrs. Thomas said. "When Mr. Alexander returns, you won't be alone in facing his questions. I promise to let him know this was my decision."

She turned and started up the stairs, Julia skipping along behind her. Mary followed them to her new room, her unease dissipating now that the housekeeper also knew the truth and was willing to help her. It felt good not having to worry about where to sleep tonight or how to provide for her needs.

Her heart lightened further as Mrs. Thomas offered to heat water for her to bathe. Perhaps things were finally working in her favor. Mary knew she'd be able to act as governess. She was educated, hardworking, and Julia seemed a sweet child. There would be no problems there.

She'd just have to convince Julia's father to keep her on, at least until such a time that she figured out what to do with her life. However, even though she didn't know the man, that didn't sound like it would be difficult at all to do. Mrs. Thomas almost made it sound as though he'd welcome her eagerly.

Chapter 6

Three days later

"Send this message to each of the addresses listed here," Simon said, sliding the paper across to the telegraph operator.

"Sure will," the man promised.

After setting his money on the counter, Simon picked up his bags and strode to the stagecoach station. The coach would be boarding in about ten minutes, and he'd be home well before nightfall. He was looking forward to it. Simon didn't really enjoy travel, much preferring to be in his own bed with meals cooked by someone he knew did a good job.

Meals. It would be past dinner by the time he got home. Perhaps he should have sent word to Mrs. Thomas and

Julia yesterday, but Simon hadn't. Instead, he planned to surprise them.

It would be nice to be back with his daughter. He could almost imagine how excited she'd be to see him. Due to multiple transportation issues, he wasn't able to do his usual visit to each of the banks he'd intended. Instead, he'd be trying again the following month. He couldn't say as he was disappointed.

Simon took a quick glance inside his travel bag to be sure the small doll he'd gotten Julia and the tin of sweets for the housekeeper were there. He smiled, thinking how delighted Julia would be with the new doll he was bringing her. This one was wearing a blue dress, and had dark hair, much like Julia's.

The sound of the stagecoach arriving snapped his attention back to the present, and he handed over his bags, then climbed inside.

With the late stage, only one other man was present, and they nodded once in greeting, then opened their respective newspapers, reading to pass the time.

Though he tried to read the latest news, Simon found his mind wandering back to thoughts of a governess when his eyes fell upon the employment ads. He frowned. He'd forgotten all about it until just now. Had Julia?

Would he be peppered with questions about one when he returned? Or would the fascination be forgotten? He hoped the latter. It wasn't that he wanted to break his daughter's heart—indeed, he'd give her most anything she wanted—it was simply that not having one would be for her own good.

Hopefully, one day she'd realize that.

Mrs. Thomas, though she might disapprove, wouldn't say much. After all, he was her employer. She'd give him a sour look, press her lips together and mutter as she walked away, but she wouldn't say anything or bring it up again.

The stagecoach started to slow, and Simon was surprised to see they were almost to town. The time had passed quickly. He must have been lost in his thoughts longer than he realized.

He pushed his concern about a governess away. He'd simply say no, and that would be that. If asked again, he'd tell them that he was no longer entertaining the idea.

"Welcome back," the stationmaster said as he opened the stage door.

"Thank you, Bobby," he said, taking his bags.

"Would you like a ride back to your home?" the man asked. "Jim's nearby."

Simon started to say he'd be fine walking, but arriving sooner would be nice. He was hungry, and hoped to find a little dinner left. "I'd welcome that," he said.

"Let me get him," the stationmaster said.

A few moments later, Simon was putting his bags into the back of Jim's wagon.

"How are you?" Simon asked. "Been busy today?"

"Not too much," Jim told him. "Though I've been in town a little more, I admit. Have been hoping to find out what happened to the young woman I drove a few days ago."

"Oh?" Simon asked.

"Strange thing, that was," Jim said. "Arrived to marry a man. Drove her out there. The woman was so excited. They'd been promised to the other for quite some time, she said. I get her out there, and you know what happened?"

"I don't, but I'm sensing it wasn't a happy ending," Simon said. "I hope he hadn't passed away."

"Worse. He had another woman hanging all over him. I took her right back to town. Pretty young woman, too. She asked if I knew where she could find work. I made a few suggestions, so I'm hoping she found something. Bobby said he didn't see her leaving on the stage, so could be she didn't have the price of the fare."

"That's terrible," Simon said. "I don't even know her and I feel badly for her situation."

Jim nodded. "That's why I'm keeping an eye out for her. Been right worried. I wanted to make sure she was—why! There she is!"

Simon looked over. They were approaching his house, and outside of it, he could see Julia on her swing. A lovely young woman stood behind her, pushing her gently. Both of them were laughing. Julia had never looked so happy, and something about that twinged at his conscience.

Simon narrowed his eyes slightly, trying to get a better look at the stranger. The woman looked slightly familiar. She...she was the one he'd bumped into when he was leaving town.

Why was she here? And with his daughter? He would figure it out and put a stop to whatever scheme she had. Had she lied to Jim? Asked him for the houses where there was wealth and children to perhaps exploit? Women were not incapable of such things. A sad story like she had could have been fabricated. The man Jim had witnessed could have been her partner in whatever crime they intended.

"Guess you hired her," Jim said, a touch of relief in his voice. "I can stop worrying now. See you later, Simon."

"Uh, yes, good day," Simon said, retrieving his bag.

"Papa!" Julia shrieked, dragging her feet to slow the swing. "You are home so early!"

A moment later, she was in his arms, hugging him tightly. "It's good to see you," he told her, looking her over closely. Were there marks on her?

Simon looked up to see the woman by the swing watching them nervously. She seemed unsure if she should approach them. Good. Let her be concerned. She had no right to be there on his property, with his daughter.

"Who is this?" he asked, trying to hide the tension in his voice. "And where is Mrs. Thomas?"

"She is baking cookies," Julia said. She glanced over her shoulder, then lowered her gaze to her shoes. "That's Mary."

"Mary." His voice was flat. "Why is she here?"

"She's...she's my friend," Julia said. "And my governess."

He tensed. What lies had this woman been telling his impressionable daughter? Simon put an arm around his daughter. "Go inside and fetch Mrs. Thomas. But you are to stay inside, do you understand? I want to talk to Mary and Mrs. Thomas."

Julia nodded, the excited look she'd worn when she first saw him now gone, replaced by one of apprehension. She slowly walked toward the house, and Simon approached the woman who still watched him, anger filling every inch of him.

"H-hello," the woman, Mary, said.

Simon didn't answer. Instead, he studied her for a moment. She was dressed in a simple gray dress, her hair pulled into a low bun at her neck. Her eyes were hazel, her hair nearly as dark as Julia's.

He wasn't sure how to address her. What to ask. Anger burned hot in him, along with fear for his daughter. But he could be—would be—rational. Calm. Try to be understanding.

However, the tone that came from his lips was anything but. "Who are you? You know as well as I do that I did not hire you to be a governess or anything else here. What lies have you been telling my daughter?"

Chapter 7

The vitriol in Julia's father's eyes sent Mary stepping backward. She'd never seen such anger before, not even the time she'd accidentally spilled ash from the fireplace on Mrs. Miles's white slippers. Her breath caught as the frightened words tried to release. "I'm-I'm not..."

It was useless, she was so frightened she couldn't speak. Her whole body trembled. Mary glanced around, wishing for help to know what to do. The way Julia had talked about her father, she'd expected a kind man. The one who stood before her seemed anything but.

"I did not intend for my daughter to have a governess," the man said. "And here you are, acting as one. A stranger, in my home and near my daughter. I deserve an answer."

Something in Mary suddenly filled her with courage. Perhaps it was an anger of her own, after the difficult few days she'd had. Maybe it was just simply tiredness at the whole situation. After all, she'd been treated so poorly by Cal, she didn't need this man doing the same. It was time to stand up for herself.

"I am not here to harm your daughter," she said firmly. "In fact, quite the opposite. I found her, lost and frightened, and brought her back here."

Something flickered over his face, and Mary wondered if his anger had been holding fear in check. "You found her?" he asked, almost uncertainly. The heat had left his voice. "Where? She was to remain with Mrs. Thomas at all times." His gaze narrowed. "Is this another lie?"

"She'd run after you to tell you goodbye," Mary said. "At least, that's what she told me. I found her in the town, and she wasn't sure how to get back home. I didn't think it was safe to just leave her, so I brought her back here, once a man gave directions. Julia told him I was her governess when he asked. I do not know why. Perhaps it was simply wishful thinking on her part. But I brought her home, and..."

She stopped then. Should she continue with the story? Mary twisted her hands together. He hadn't interrupted her, so she said, "Well, once more, Julia called me a governess, to Mrs. Thomas. They were both so excited I was here."

"I imagine so," he muttered. "Go on."

"But I never lied," Mary said, raising her chin. "I explained what had happened, and why I was here. That I was seeking employment. Mrs. Thomas said she couldn't offer me a position, but suggested I stay on until you arrived, and see if you'd be interested in my help."

Julia's father studied her for an agonizing moment. She felt anxious, worried he might accuse her of lying again. She had the feeling that no matter how she defended herself, he wouldn't believe her. But, to her surprise, he let out a sigh and shook his head.

"I might have known," he said. "Of course she would offer that. Mrs. Thomas wants Julia to have a governess as much as Julia wants one."

"I...I've not had experience being a governess," Mary admitted, "but I've good references from a family I worked for previously as a housemaid. I am also educated. As I told Mrs. Thomas, I also can help with cooking and sew. I've made many dresses for little girls and their dolls."

Julia's father didn't speak, but his lips were pressed together and his arms folded across his chest. When he didn't reply, she took that as a dismissal.

"I'll leave," Mary said, her voice quiet. "I've no wish to be where I'm not wanted. If it's of any importance to you, I've neither taken nor expected a wage for my time here. The bed and meals were enough in trade for taking care of Julia. However, since you had no intention of hiring someone at all, I'll pay you back for those. Just tell me what I owe you."

A small frown crept across his face. "You don't need to do that. However, humor me. Just how did you take care of Julia?"

"I've not been here for long," Mary said, "but we did her lessons together and read. She drew in her sketchbook, and we spent time in the garden, looking at the plants and helping care for them. Mrs. Thomas allowed us in the kitchen to make a cake, and we used her mathematical lessons to practice measurements and simple arithmetic. This evening, I'd also planned to teach her some simple stitches so that she could make a dress for her doll."

"I see."

Mary turned toward the house, but then paused. "I'll get my bags," she told him. "But I want you to know, I'd never hurt Julia. She's a lovely girl, sweet, clever, but also lonely and in need of friendship. That's all I was trying to be. A friend."

The door to the house opened, and Mrs. Thomas, worry on her face, and Julia, tears on her cheeks, came rushing toward them.

"Don't go!" Julia shrieked. "Papa, don't make her go!"

Mary wasn't sure why, after all, she hardly knew the little girl, but something about how she pleaded, grabbing on to her and then to her father, made Mary's eyes widen. Was it that she felt sympathy for the girl's sorrow? Or was it fear, at the realization that once she did leave, she had nowhere to go? Mary could take the stagecoach somewhere, but she didn't know how far her funds would take her or how to choose a town where there might be opportunity for her.

She couldn't go back to Mrs. Miles. There was no family wondering about her. All she had she'd sold or brought, thinking that she and Cal would marry, meaning that she had nothing with which to set up a home of her own. And she'd never, never go to Cal and beg for help. It still galled her that his parting words had been asking about *her* money.

Mary closed her eyes a moment. It didn't matter. She'd figure things out. Women had to do that sort of thing when they had no one else. She would be no different.

Chapter 8

"No!" Julia cried out. "Please, Papa! Don't make her go!"

Simon watched as Mrs. Thomas quickly put a hand on Julia's shoulder. "Mr. Alexander," she said, "I'm to blame in this situation, as I'd allowed Mary to stay. But, though she's only been here a few days..." the housekeeper stopped, and her eyes darted between all of the involved parties.

He closed his eyes for a moment and let out a small sigh of frustration. This was the last thing he wanted. Coming home after a trip that hadn't gone as planned, finding a strange—and beautiful—woman there, and now, his daughter upset and Mrs. Thomas looking as though she was disapproving of him.

"I don't like this situation," he admitted. "I feel as though I was tricked, and now I'm being ganged up on."

"That's not our intention," Mrs. Thomas said quietly.

"I know it's not," Simon answered. "It's just how I feel." He carefully studied each of the females.

Julia was looking anxious, her small hands twisting together. Mrs. Thomas looked conflicted, as though she wished to say more, and Mary, she had a mixture of fear and worry on her face.

He tried to think about how each of them felt. Put himself in their shoes, as it were. It would only be the fair thing to do. Julia, of course she wanted a governess. She wanted someone to play with her, to be a companion. So, he understood why she'd done what she had. The housekeeper, well, he understood her position as well. She had a great deal to do running the household, and couldn't do it while giving a young girl all the attention she needed.

While she'd been taking care of both Julia and the home for years, it was vastly different, an infant who could be contained and a young, restless girl, with a mind full of imagination and longing to learn more of the world about her. His daughter was bright and curious. Was he doing the right thing by keeping her to himself? Her protection was his goal, but...

As for Mary...he stared at her the longest. If she noticed, he wasn't sure. She was looking down at her shoes right now. What would it be like to move to a new town, one where the only one you knew was the man who'd promised to marry you, but then didn't wait? If the story was true. It was likely a relief to be offered a bed and food in trade for work. If Mrs. Thomas hadn't taken her in, where would she have slept? What would she have eaten? It was possible she had little in the way of money, if any.

Not a fair situation, though, bed and meals only in trade for work. But if she was desperate, and he could see how she was, it was likely a lifeline she'd clung to, until she could figure out what she was to do now.

But the fact remained. She was a stranger, and he'd done all he could to protect his daughter from anyone who might do her harm, physically or emotionally. Simon could see she already bore affection for Mary. He didn't like that. That kind of attention should have been for her mother, Meghan. Who was no longer with them. Could he fault his daughter for clinging to another woman? One younger than Mrs. Thomas, one who might be a mother?

"Perhaps you'd best go to your room," Mrs. Thomas told Julia quietly.

His daughter nodded. She ran over to Mary, and said in a trembling voice, "Don't leave until you tell me goodbye."

There was dampness on Mary's cheeks, and she nodded, as she held his daughter for a long moment. He didn't miss the obvious affection between the two.

Julia went to him next. "Papa," she whispered as she held his larger hands in her two, "I don't want Mary to replace Mama. I just want her just because she's...her."

She ran off then before he could say anything, but Simon nearly staggered back, one hand pressing into his heart. How had she...? Quickly, Simon regained control of his emotions.

"Mrs. Thomas," he said. "What exactly did you offer?"

"A bed and meals," the housekeeper answered, "and then to let the two of you work things out upon your return."

He nodded. In truth, he wished the woman had told Mary a set number of days. That would have made this whole thing easier. If he gave in, and allowed her to stay, could he live with himself if she turned out to be far different from how she presented herself?

"We had thought you would be gone for several weeks longer," Mrs. Thomas admitted. "Then I'd have had a better report for you on how Mary was doing with Julia. A trial, if you will." She stepped closer. "You must know, I'd have never allowed her to be alone with Julia unless she had a reference. She does, and I saw it. She insisted I did, and it is excellent."

"Then that is what we will do," Simon found himself saying. "A trial period. It would only be fair, since I assume you were hoping for such a thing while you figured out what you were going to do in the future," he said, addressing Mary.

"If you'd rather I be a house or a kitchen maid," the woman quickly offered, "or know of someone who does need one, just until I—"

He shook his head. "No. Perhaps it is time I consider a governess for Julia. If that will be you, I can't say, but I owe it to all of us, myself included, to at least try this experiment."

"Thank you," Mary said, meeting his eyes shyly and offering the first smile he'd seen since he'd spoken to her, even if it was a tentative one.

A warmth spread through him, and Simon quickly looked away. He couldn't allow that feeling. Would never allow those tendrils of something he hadn't felt for so long to wrap their way around his soul.

Mrs. Thomas returned to the house, Mary following her. From the second floor window, Simon felt sure that his daughter was watching. In truth, he'd always felt a little outnumbered as the only male in the house. Adding another female might only lead to disaster.

Or, it might lead to more, a small voice whispered.

But Simon tensed, shook his head, and picked up his bags. No, no, it wouldn't. Without Meghan, he'd never have anything more than what he had now. His beautiful daughter he was trying to raise, and endless heartache.

Simon walked inside and climbed the stairs to his room to set his bags down. He was too tired to unpack, but he took a moment to wash his face and hands. Deciding to check in on Julia, he neared her room and paused, just out of sight, listening, watching.

Her door was open, and Julia was reading aloud from a book. She paused, and asked, "Why do you think that is?"

He hadn't heard the start of the paragraph to know what she was referring to, but he could see Mary's thoughtful expression on her face, as she slowly said, "I think, perhaps, because all parents, animal kingdom or not, love their children dearly and want to protect them."

Simon tensed, waiting to hear what Julia would say next.

"Papa would protect me," Julia agreed. "Would your parents?"

"I...I suppose they would," Mary answered, her voice soft. It grew stronger, as she said, "But I don't have parents anymore, so I just have to guess."

"You are like me," Julia said. "No mama."

"I am," Mary agreed, in a matter-of-fact way. Then she added, "But even if someone doesn't have a mother or a father, because that time does come for everyone, those people aren't gone forever. There are many ways to keep them alive in our hearts."

Simon cleared his throat. This wasn't the sort of thing he wanted to hear. His noise had the desired effect. Mary stopped talking, and Julia frowned in thought, and returned to her book.

He strode past. Despite her trying to be kind to Julia, he knew Mary was very wrong. The only way to ensure the memory of someone was to lock it closely away. Talking about them, thinking about them, it only led to pain. Something he'd had quite enough of, and something he wanted to spare his daughter from. He'd have to speak to Mary about avoiding the topics he didn't want Julia to think about.

Chapter 9

Mary awoke with a gasp as she glanced around the unfamiliar room. Then she relaxed, remembering where she was. At the Alexander house, in a room that was simply beautiful, with a large window, a comfortable bed, and...and an angry man nearby.

She'd been surprised that Mr. Alexander had allowed her to stay. He'd even told her that evening before she retired that he'd pay a fair wage. She was grateful for that. Every penny would be needed in order to figure out her future.

Mrs. Thomas had hinted there might be other men in search of a bride in the area and that she'd be glad to introduce her around, but Mary was sure she didn't want to live anywhere near Cal. She also wanted—perhaps most importantly—a man to choose her for herself, not because he needed a female to cook and clean.

Maybe she could revive her old dream of creating matching children's and doll's dresses. Why not? The only thing was, she'd need to move to a larger town. One where there would be wealthier individuals, and a good number in the population, in order to improve her chances at clients. She could get a little shop, live over it, and start anew.

Tinges of sadness started to overcome Mary. She was tired of always starting over, but it seemed that was her situation at present. However, thinking about it wasn't making things better. It was time to just get on with the day.

Quickly, she rose and dressed, and then knocked at Julia's door. "It's time to get up," she said.

"I'm awake," the girl called out.

Mary headed toward the stairs, and went into the kitchen. Mrs. Thomas was bustling around, and the smell of fresh biscuits hung in the air.

"Good morning," Mrs. Thomas said. "Take those to the table?"

"Of course," Mary said, taking the biscuits, then returning for a pot of strawberry jam and a large pat of butter.

Mr. Alexander walked in. He nodded to her, and then sat at the table just as Julia walked in. She took the chair beside her father, and Mary hesitated, not sure if she should sit with them, as she'd done yesterday, or if she should move into the kitchen.

Luckily, Mrs. Thomas came out just then. "Let's eat while it's warm," she said, setting down bowls of oatmeal, and putting herself in a chair.

Mary sat, and helped herself once the others had, still feeling nervous.

"What are your plans today with Julia?" her father asked.

"Since she has no schoolwork today," Mary said, "a walk or two around the grounds, and perhaps a game, and read. We'll practice a few more sewing stitches too."

He nodded in satisfaction. "Fine, fine."

"I need to get a few things in town," Mrs. Thomas said. "Mary, would you like to accompany me? Julia can join us, and we can show you around."

"I would love to, if that's all right with you, Mr. Alexander?" Mary ventured.

"Simon," he said. "Simon is fine. And yes, I suppose so. Julia, you are to stay right with Mrs. Thomas." He hesitated. "And Mary."

Julia nodded. "Yes, Papa. What are you doing today?"

"Work, little one. I will go into the bank and spend some time there." Her father tugged on Julia's long braid. "Speaking of, I'd best get started."

He excused himself from the table, and Mary couldn't help but feel just a little bit relieved as he left.

"You'll feel more at home soon," Mrs. Thomas said over her teacup. "He's not really so bad. Why don't we get ready to leave?"

"I'm sure you are right," Mary answered. As she stood, she added, "I look forward to it. Julia, can you get yourself washed before we go?"

The girl nodded, and it wasn't long before the three of them were walking toward town. Mrs. Thomas pointed out the different buildings and told Mary a little about each of the people who ran them. It was on the tip of Mary's tongue to inquire about the opportunity to be a dressmaker, but aside from the fact she didn't want to live so closely to Cal, it seemed possible the people who lived here likely wouldn't have the extra funds. Most of them looked as though they were like her, starting from scratch.

Julia was skipping along, seemingly happy to be in town. "Papa gave me a nickel," she announced suddenly. "Might we stop in the general store?"

"Of course," Mrs. Thomas said. "It's right over here, Mary. And one of the stops I needed to make."

Mary followed Mrs. Thomas and Julia inside the general store, and looked around appreciatively. She hadn't been sure what to expect, this far west where it was harder to get supplies, but the store was well stocked with dry goods, such as beans, coffee, sugar, flour, and cornmeal, as well as fabrics, soaps, sweets, and household goods.

As her eye landed on a quilt someone had made and put up for sale, a pang of wistfulness washed over her. It was the same blue as the one she'd made so long ago, but instead of stars decorating the cover, this one had squares. Mary stroked it gently.

"Lovely, isn't it?" Mrs. Thomas said, coming next to her.

"Yes," Mary agreed. "It's similar to one I made last year."

"Did you bring it with you?" the housekeeper asked. "You can place it on your bed."

"No, I had to sell it. I didn't have room and...and..." Mary wasn't surprised the tears came to her eyes, "I'm not sure now, seeing this one, I could ever make a quilt such a color again. It reminds me of all I've lost."

"All you've been spared from," Mrs. Thomas said gently. "I much prefer yellow or lavender, don't you?"

"Yes," Mary said, raising her chin. "I only chose blue since Cal liked it."

"Even better you no longer have it—or him," Mrs. Thomas said.

Mary smiled at her gratefully. "Thank you," she whispered. "You've made me feel better."

The older woman gave her a gentle squeeze on her arm and then walked away. Mary took a deep breath and then resumed walking around the store. There was nothing she needed, and she didn't have much to spend with her, but perhaps one day.

The door to the store opened, and a man walked in. Mary couldn't see who he was and looked away, not really caring. It wasn't like she knew many people in the town to be polite and say hello to.

The man stepped to the counter, and she could hear the general store owner saying, "I'm sorry, Mr. Lynch."

Mr. Lynch? Mary's eyes widened, and she ducked behind a display of books. Likely the last place Cal would look in the store.

"Come on, you've got to give me more credit." Cal's voice filled the store. He wasn't angry, more pleading.

"You've already got a credit of twenty dollars that's past due. I can't give you any more beyond that. I have a business to run," the general store owner said.

"Then what am I supposed to do? Starve?" Cal growled.

"Get a job," the owner said, his voice firm. "Stop playing cards. There's not many you don't owe in this town. Work, and you can pay us back."

Mary's heart thudded, and she quickly turned away, stooping even lower as Cal stormed out of the store.

He hadn't seen her, of that she was sure, but she stayed there, shaking, and trying to catch her breath for a moment.

Mrs. Thomas came around the corner, and in a low voice said, "Mary, are you hiding from that man?"

"That's him," Mary squeaked. "The man I was to be wedded to." She stood just tall enough to peer through a window to be sure he wasn't nearby and twisted her hands together. "I shouldn't have hidden, I've done no wrong, but..."

"I understand," Mrs. Thomas said. She shook her head slowly. "My girl, he doesn't sound like a good man at all. Playing cards? Finding himself in debt? Not to mention how he left you, and got another woman with child."

"I had no idea, not any of those things," Mary said. "You must believe me. I'm not the sort of a person to associate with a man like that."

The housekeeper nodded. "I know." She turned and looked around for Julia. "Julia, I think it's going to rain. We should leave. Have you chosen what you want?"

"I have!" Julia walked up to the counter. "Mr. Charles, might I have a bit of pink ribbon, and with whatever is left, can you get me a candy stick?"

"I sure can," the shop owner said. He cut a generous length of pink ribbon, placed it carefully in a bit of brown paper, and then put a pink candy stick in another bit of paper, pushing them over to the girl.

Julia proudly handed him her nickel, and stepped back, allowing Mrs. Thomas to purchase the items she had in her basket. Mary was so distracted, peering out the window, she didn't see what was bought.

"Let's go," the housekeeper said briskly a moment later, leading the way through the door. "That sky doesn't look friendly."

Mary glanced up. She'd thought it was perhaps an excuse Mrs. Thomas had made to help them leave town, but it appeared she was right. The sky was gray, and thick clouds filled it. The air felt oppressive, though Mary wasn't sure if it really did, or if that was her apprehension at running into Cal.

As she, Mrs. Thomas, and Julia scurried back to the house, a smattering of raindrops accompanying them on the journey, all she could think about was the terrible situation she was in. It had been foolish to hope she wouldn't run into Cal. He was here, a far different man than she'd thought, and something made her wonder if he found her, if he'd somehow force her to give him all the money she had, money she'd promised to bring when she arrived. If he did ask, what would she do? That was all she had. Mary was determined not to spend any of it, since she didn't know what the future would hold.

Despite the warm air, when they reached the house and took shelter moments before the sky broke open, Mary found herself with goosebumps all over her. Not from the wind, but from fear.

Chapter 10

Simon glanced up from the small table he'd settled himself at inside the bank. The single teller window with bars over it was empty on the customer side. On the employee side, Max Duncan, his teller, sat carefully thumbing through the pages of a ledger that recorded loan payments.

A storm had just come through, so fierce for a time the small building had shuddered. That was why it was so quiet. It was only now that the townsfolk were venturing outside again.

"How does it all look?" Simon asked. "I've not had a chance to go over it this month."

"Everyone's made payments on time," Max answered. Then he added, "Which isn't a surprise, seeing as the bank is careful who it loans to."

"We have to be," Simon said grimly. "It's more than reputation at stake. It's the folks who depend on us to be here in town, something we wouldn't be able to be if we didn't have money flowing in and out. That's why some banks fail."

Simon was grateful that not a single bank he oversaw had problems with loans, thefts, or poor employees. He prided himself on being fair and reasonable, but tolerating no misbehavior at all.

"It's real nice of you to come in here while Mick's taking a trip so I'm not alone," Max said.

"I'm happy to do it. Besides, though I doubt we'd have problems in our little town, we sure don't want to risk it. Having just one man here alone is asking for trouble. Even if the sheriff is next door."

"I agree," Max said. Then he frowned. "And might be here comes some now."

"Oh?" Simon rose, and joined Max at the window.

A man was heading toward the bank, looking nervous. He also looked average. Moderately good looks, medium build, looked as though he generally kept himself groomed. But there was something about him, almost a presence that surrounded him, that made Simon tense slightly.

"That man came in here just the other day, wanting a loan," Max said quietly. "But before he could tell us why, someone invited him to a card game and he left. I'm not saying that's why he wanted the money, but..."

"I trust your instincts," Simon said, his eyes not leaving the man who was now almost to the bank door. "Let's see if he comes in."

Sure enough, the man walked in, and headed straight toward the counter. "I'm here to see about a loan," he said confidently.

"I'll handle this," Simon said, nodding at Max. "Mister?"

"Lynch. Cal Lynch," the man answered. "I need a loan." He wet his lips. "Have had some unexpected expenses, and a woman in the family way."

"I see," Simon said. "Congratulations, Mr. Lynch." He studied the man before him, whose eyes were darting everywhere but at him. "Now, I must tell you, the bank doesn't loan money to everyone who asks, but let's see if we can help you. What do you have for collateral?"

"Got a homestead; just a few more years it's mine." Cal squinted at him then. "That good enough?"

"I'm afraid not," Simon said, trying to force regret in his tone. "The land isn't yours yet. Do you have anything else? Horses? Cattle?"

Cal scratched his head. "Not really." Then he perked up. "But, I promise, it will be paid back. I'm a man of my word."

"I'm sure you are, Mr. Lynch," Simon said, "but the bank's rules are we need collateral. An assurance of repayment."

The man frowned and tapped at his cheek. "Just a small loan then? Maybe I can win a few hands of cards at the saloon, triple it."

Simon winced, and tried to hide the reaction. "We don't give loans for gambling, I'm afraid."

The man scowled. "Then how am I supposed to get money?"

"Perhaps someone is hiring," Simon offered. "Have you checked around town?"

"Nah, I'm not interested in work," Cal said. He drummed his fingers on the counter, and the sound irritated Simon. "Maybe...say, can I take a loan out in my intended's name? Well, she's not my intended anymore."

"Oh, your wife?" Simon asked. "Perhaps."

The man shook his head. "No, we aren't getting married. But she promised me when she came, she'd give me all her wages from when she was working before we married. A promise is a promise, and I intend to collect. Can you believe she rode off without giving me a dime? It's mine! She'd said so in a letter."

Simon stilled. It was difficult to follow along, but if Cal Lynch was saying what he seemed to be...well, he couldn't believe the words coming from this man. Finally, he shook his head. "Forgive me, but I'm not quite understanding."

"I was going to marry a woman," Cal explained. "We got promised before I came out here and got the land. She stayed back, working. I met someone else here. She's the one who's going to have my baby."

"And you think the woman you'd left behind is still going to give you money?" Simon asked doubtfully. What kind of person would do such a thing? None that he knew. The man's case for getting a loan was growing weaker by the moment. What in the world had made him think he could walk in, with no resources or collateral, and get a loan? Especially when he'd already stated he didn't want to work and alluded to the fact he'd use it for gambling.

The man shrugged. "A promise is a promise," he said. "And she told me she was bringing money. Besides, she might do it, just to get rid of me. Or..." A thoughtful look came over his face. "Maybe Mary will let me win her back. Just long enough to get the money, you see."

"Mary?" Simon asked, stilling.

"That's right. Mary Clinton. She's here, somewhere. I know she didn't leave. I just have to find where she's hiding herself," Cal said.

Simon felt a strange lurch in his stomach. If his suspicions were correct, for just how many Mary Clintons could there be in this town, the man before him was talking about his new governess. This was the man Mary had come to marry? The idea was shocking. How could she have been so desperate?

The man didn't seem the marrying sort, nor did he seem honest. This meant that Mary had been, for surely no one could be so stupid as to have Cal as an accomplice. The man seemed quite open and vocal about his life, regardless of how it made him look.

"I'm sorry," Simon finally said. "I'll need property of some sort; a promise of repayment isn't enough without collateral. If you can find such a thing, I'll consider it. But I have to abide by the bank's rules."

"Sure, sure," Cal muttered, walking away.

Simon's eyes followed him as he walked toward the saloon and pushed open the swinging door. Now that the man was gone, he let himself fill with the fury he'd been trying to tamp down.

And the worry.

What if this man found his way to his home? Bothered his daughter? All because of the woman—who he'd never wanted as a governess—living there. Worry was warring with disgust over the man.

"About closing time," Max said with a sigh of relief. "I always like these half days on Saturday."

"So do I," Simon agreed. "I don't think we'll get anyone else. I'm going to go ahead and lock the front door. When you are ready, we will leave."

In short work, the doors were locked, the money secured, and the ledgers also in a safe box. Simon bid Max farewell, and began the walk toward home.

He wondered if Cal Lynch would be looking for him, following him. He doubted it, however. The man hadn't even met his eyes once during their conversation, so he doubted that he knew what Simon looked like. Still, he felt a little uneasy.

Was that in part because he didn't like the man instinctively, what he'd done to Mary notwithstanding? Or was it because of how the man had spoken about trying to get back with Mary? Would she really take him back? The man seemed—

It was none of his concern. Simon hardly knew Mary.

So why was it that he felt worry? Beyond what would just be that of a friendly concern? Maybe it was because she seemed not only a practical woman but also kind.

Lovely.

Why did the image of Mary in Cal Lynch's arms upset him? Make his stomach churn? Cause his heart to speed up in a way that made him feel sick? Simon wasn't sure, but he also refused to let himself think anything more about it.

When he reached home a few moments later, he nodded hello to Mrs. Thomas, and headed toward his study.

"Mr. Alexander," she called.

He stopped. "What is it?"

The housekeeper's hands were twisted together, and he could feel the nervousness radiating off of her. "Is Julia all right?" he asked, moving toward the stairs to check on her.

"She's fine," the housekeeper said firmly, stopping him. "Spent her nickel on a new ribbon and a stick of candy."

He nodded. That was all right then. So, what was the problem? He frowned. "Is Mary—" He stopped. How could he ask if she was doing her job properly? Or if she was unwell. Perhaps she'd even run off! Impatiently, he asked, "What is the problem?"

"It has to do with Mary, in a way," the housekeeper said. Before his frown could grow, she added, "When we were at the general store, that man who she was to marry came in. Poor woman looked so frightened, I saw her hiding."

"Is that so?" Simon asked. He sighed and said, "I don't want trouble here, especially not around Julia. I wonder if she should leave."

"You can't send her away," Mrs. Thomas protested, her face growing hot with anger she was trying to keep in check. "Not after promising a trial. Besides, it's not the poor woman's fault. You are a man, Mr. Alexander. You don't understand how often women have no say and no control over what happens in a relationship. You are one of the rare ones, in what we see is what we get. Not all men are so honest. A good number are scoundrels."

He knew she was right, but he hesitated to answer. It very well could have been that Mary knew that's how the man was, and still accepted his proposal. Instead, he asked, "What happened in the store? Other than Mary getting distressed?"

The woman frowned, and her eyes blazed with the likes of which Simon couldn't recall he'd ever seen. "He has a debt at the general store. Sounded to me like debts all over. Possibly a gambling problem."

Simon glanced around, and then held a finger to his lips. He pointed to his study, and Mrs. Thomas followed him curiously. Once she was inside, he closed the door most of the way.

"A Cal Lynch came into the bank, wanting a loan," Simon said, his voice low. "He said that Mary was good for paying it. He also said something else."

The housekeeper gasped, and her hands flew over her mouth. "That man!" she fumed. "What did he say?"

"He insinuated that he was going to look for her, to make her get back with him so he could have the money she'd brought for their future."

"Oh! You can't let him!" Mrs. Thomas cried out. "That poor girl! She's worked so hard. She needs to keep that, to figure out whatever her future will hold." The woman began to pace. "I cannot believe this. Why, you have to tell her, Mr. Alexander. This can't be kept secret."

"I will," he assured her. "But I have to do some work first. I'll speak with her later. In the meantime, you know my feelings have not changed about strangers around my home. I regret allowing Mary here because of that man. I expect you to keep a close eye out for trouble."

"I will," the housekeeper promised. She met his eyes. "But I think you've nothing to worry about with Mary. She seems a good one, and dare I also say, the sort of person that you need."

Simon would have answered that he doubted that, or perhaps that the housekeeper should mind her own business, or one of the many other things that came to his mind in that instant, but Mrs. Thomas turned on her heel and left, swiftly closing his study door behind her.

Simon paced his study for a few moments before sitting down. Outside, the sky had grown darker again. The faint sound of thunder rumbled, and he closed his eyes for a moment, hoping that by giving in to his daughter and the housekeeper, he hadn't allowed the very thing he'd tried to keep out of there. Danger to his daughter.

Chapter 11

Rain beat against the windows, leaving trails as the drops slipped down. Julia sighed softly as she watched them.

"Are you bored?" Mary asked. "Do you want to play another game?"

"Not really," Julia admitted.

"What would you like to do then?" Mary asked. "Read? Draw?"

"No, I'd like to show you something," Julia said, sitting up suddenly. Her eyes were wide as she said softly, "But I don't want you to tell anyone."

"Why is that?" Mary asked.

"It's because..." Julia took a deep breath. "It's because it would make Papa sad." She started to blink rapidly, and Mary realized that she was trying not to cry.

"Your papa isn't keen on secrets," Mary said softly. "Is this something that could get someone hurt? Or in trouble?"

"No," Julia said, shaking her head. "I'll show you."

She jumped up and left the room, where she walked to the far end of the hallway. She stopped at a small door and opened it. Mary looked on in surprise as it led to a small flight of stairs.

"You can't stand up all the way," Julia warned her. "You might hit your head."

"Then I'll be careful," Mary said. She hadn't realized that there was a third story.

"In our attic, there are all kinds of things," Julia told her, her voice slightly muffled. "But it's not as tall as the regular floors, so it's hard to look around."

"Do you come here sometimes to play?" Mary asked. She kept one hand above her, feeling for the ceiling. She found it, then realized in gratitude she could just stand properly without striking her head. She had about two inches to spare.

"I do," Julia said. "But not when Papa is home. As he's at the bank, he won't catch me."

Mary hesitated. She wasn't sure if she should question Julia about why she wasn't allowed here. It didn't look, based on the lantern that Julia held, and the small window letting in gray light, that it was because the attic was a safety hazard. There wasn't much in here. A few trunks, some boxes, an old chair.

"Attics are interesting places," Mary remarked, picking up an old book sitting in the chair. "Sometimes they hold fascinating treasures."

"This one does," Julia said eagerly. Then she laughed. "And some funny things too! Look!" She scampered across the dusty floor and picked up an old man's hat, plopping it on her head. A gentleman's walking stick was nearby, and she picked that up as well. "Such fun clothes to dress up in," she giggled.

"Yes, indeed," Mary said. "I used to work for a family who had a very large attic. They had furniture and paintings and clothes that were more than a hundred years old up there. I enjoyed every time I was asked to put something in storage. I never knew just what I would see, but all of it was fascinating."

"This is the best of all," Julia said, taking off the hat and setting down the cane. "Come look with me."

Mary followed her a short distance away, to a small collection of items along the back wall, pausing before a few trunks. They looked quite old, but there wasn't any dust on the tops of them. In fact, there wasn't much dust up here at all, showing that someone came and went, at least occasionally.

Julia kneeled before one of the trunks, humming softly to herself and opening it as easily as though she'd done it a dozen times. Mary sat next to her and was surprised to see once the lid had raised that the trunk held an array of things inside.

There were photographs and paintings inside of frames, piles of soft fabric that looked to be dresses, and a bundle of papers. A hairbrush, with a few dark strands still, a small silver hand mirror that was turning gray along the edges, and a bottle of perfume sat inside of a small open box.

"These are my mother's," Julia whispered, almost reverently, as she ran a hand along the cloth. "I know that's her picture. It's got to be. That's Papa."

Julia picked up one of the photographs and studied it while Mary looked over her shoulder. Indeed, that was a younger Simon Alexander in it, his eyes full of love for the smiling woman next to him.

"There's none with me, since Mama died when she was having me," Julia said, her faint voice trembling, "but I come here, and I look at the pictures and I think about her. Think about how she might look at me that way and smile at me."

"I think that she would," Mary told her softly, putting a hand on Julia's small shoulder. "I never knew your mother, but I know you, and I think it quite impossible that anyone couldn't look at you and love you as much as I do, in my short time here."

The girl smiled at her, almost shyly, then said, "Look. Here's an old journal. I can't read much, though. The handwriting doesn't make sense. Yet. Maybe when I'm older I can read cursive better. Here's one of her dresses, the same one as in the photograph." The girl showed her, and indeed, it was the same.

"There's letters, from Papa, though I have trouble reading them as well. So, all of this must be my mother's." Julia picked up another of the pictures, a small painted portrait of a woman who looked very much like Julia. "We even looked the same."

"Yes, you did," Mary said softly.

"I...I wanted to show you, because this is such a special place to me," Julia said. "But I don't want Papa mad, if he knows I found these things."

"Your father must have loved your mother a great deal," Mary said. "I see it in his eyes." She gently returned the photograph to the trunk.

"But he never talks about her," Julia said, frustration clear in her voice. "How can I know who my mama was, and remember her, if he doesn't tell me?"

"That's why you come here," Mary realized. "To learn what you can."

"Yes," Julia said. "Because Papa might be willing to hide her away, but I don't want to. I want to know more about her."

"Was Mrs. Thomas around then?" Mary asked. "Perhaps she would know."

"No, she wasn't," Julia said sadly.

They were quiet for a few moments, and Mary said slowly, "I don't think your father keeps this here to make you sad or to hide her from you."

"Then why?" Julia asked, her voice almost pleading. "Why won't he talk about her?"

Mary's heart ached for the young girl. "I think," she said softly, as she brushed a strand of hair from Julia's cheek, "that he just misses her so much, it's painful for him to see these things."

"I miss her too." Julia sniffled, and leaned into Mary. "I miss her so much."

"I imagine you do," Mary said, rubbing her hand up and down the girl's back.

She didn't know what to say. She wanted to comfort her, to give a good reason for why her father had done such a thing that Julia might understand, but how could a child so young understand that sometimes, the only way that another could deal with such intense pain and loss was to try and forget about it? It was what she'd been doing with her time with Cal.

Now, she felt like she understood Simon's outburst a little more. She couldn't imagine being suddenly left alone with an infant, when the one you'd pledged your life to passed away. Just when the child you were so excited to meet, alongside of your spouse, came into the world. Of course you wouldn't want a stranger seeming to take her place.

"Will you help me?" Julia asked, pulling away slightly. Mary could see the mixture of desperation and hopefulness in her eyes. "Could you read to me from here? So I can know my mama better?"

Mary wiped at the tears on Julia's face. "I—"

"What are you doing up here?" Simon's cold voice cut through the attic, and as Mary turned, his face in the flickering lamplight was one of such pain, such anger, she started to tremble. Beside her, Julia gasped and scrambled to her feet.

"Get out," Simon said, his voice so quiet Mary could barely hear him. "Get out."

Chapter 12

Simon reached for some paper from his desk, but his hand brushed against the bare wooden bottom of the drawer. He glanced inside. Empty. Had he used the last of it already? Usually, he kept that drawer filled with paper, so he could easily access it when needed, and it didn't blow away or get crumpled.

Luckily, he had more in his room. Last week, he'd picked some up and mistakenly carried it there, intending to deposit it in his study, only to forget. He rose and left the study, wondering at the quiet in the house. Though Julia wasn't a loud child, he could usually hear her doing something. Asking questions, playing with a doll, singing softly, or the sound that pencil and paper and the turning of pages made, as she did her studies, drew, or read.

This afternoon, however, there was nothing. He knew she was home, as was Mary, since Mrs. Thomas had told them about what had happened at the general store. Since it was raining outside, they had to be here.

Curiosity filling him now, he came to the top of the stairs and headed toward his daughter's room, peering inside. It was empty. Maybe she was in the kitchen. Sometimes she went there. He'd overheard Mary talking to her about baking cookies or a cake this morning.

I'll just fetch my paper and go in the kitchen to get a drink, and see what she's doing, he thought, still not entirely comfortable with the idea of having a governess around. But first, the paper, since he was upstairs.

He went into his room and spied the bundle of paper upon a small table. As he reached for it, the sound of something above him in the attic caught his attention. Simon frowned. Was there an animal up there? Another creak sounded, and then a gentle thump, as though something were walking around.

He sighed. Last summer, a racoon had somehow gotten inside. He imagined, as large as this sounded, it had happened again. After he verified that's what it was, he'd pay for Jim to come trap it and remove the thing.

Simon moved to the hallway, setting his paper on a shelf there, and then went to the door leading to the attic stairs, a small lantern in hand. He half wondered if he should fetch the broom to defend himself, but decided he'd just take a quick peek. Just enough to see the critter.

Just as he neared the top, Simon stilled upon hearing voices. His jaw clenched. That was no wild animal in his attic. It was the governess. And his daughter.

He tried to tell himself to wait before jumping to conclusions, but Julia knew she wasn't allowed up here. Perhaps Mary hadn't realized that. Or had it been her idea to explore? Maybe his daughter was innocent in all of this.

He took two more steps, and then froze, as he could hear their voices more clearly.

"Could you read to me from here? So I can know my mama better?" Julia was asking.

Meghan's trunks! Her letters? Journal? Simon flew up the remaining steps. He had to preserve them. Couldn't let anything happen to what little he had left of Meghan.

He got to the top of the stairs and took in the scene before him. One of the trunks was open, and Julia and Mary were kneeling in front of it, looking at the photographs. Mary's arm was around his daughter.

Anger filled him. But it was more than that. It was. Fear. Every inch of him felt fearful. Had anything been hurt? Disturbed? Were the pictures damaged?

"What are you doing up here?" he asked, not recognizing his voice as it cut through their soft conversation.

Julia's eyes were wide, filled with fear as she hurried to her feet.

"Get out," Simon said, his voice so quiet he could hardly hear himself. His words were directed toward Mary, though it was Julia who stepped closer toward the exit.

The words had been hard, and he regretted them as soon as they escaped. Why was it around Mary he got so angry? So irrational?

What he meant, he wasn't sure. Out of the attic, yes. Out of his home? Probably. The woman had done nothing but cause problems since she'd arrived.

But...

No, that wasn't true. She hadn't. It's just...he didn't want her here. Not among Meghan's things.

His eyes locked on the photograph of his wife, peeking from the top of the trunk, and he spoke again. "Get out."

"I, I didn't—" Julia's voice was pitched slightly higher than usual.

Simon didn't even look at her. He couldn't tear his eyes away from the trunk, and the hope that nothing had been disturbed. "Go to your room," he ordered.

He was aware that Julia moved past him, was aware of Mary's wary expression, one of apprehension. Worry. But that didn't matter.

"What have you touched?" he asked, carefully resting a hand on the trunk. "Did she take anything? Is anything damaged?"

Simon was aware, suddenly, that his hands were trembling. Was it rage? Fear? Sorrow? Why was it all of those emotions elicited the exact same response? He wasn't sure, but he couldn't help but wish that things were as they'd been years before. When he was happy. Smiled. Laughed. When was the last time he'd done that? He couldn't remember. All he knew was there was no reason to do so. Seeing his smiling face from years long gone made him ache.

"Nothing was hurt," Mary said quietly. "Julia showed me the trunks. She showed me the photographs, and we looked at those. Other than her touching the dress and photos, and showing me the book inside, she touched nothing else, and she was very gentle."

He nodded, sure that was the truth as it didn't look like anything was disturbed or damaged. Simon carefully repacked the items, unable to stop his fingers from lingering. As he latched the trunk once more, he turned to Mary. She was still watching him.

"I'm sorry," he started, unsure if he should continue with a real apology, or tell her that under no uncertain terms should she or Julia ever look at these again.

"Your wife was beautiful," she said, not waiting for him to speak.

He sucked in a breath sharply. "Yes. She was. Both inside and out." His eyes prickled, and he drew in a shuddering breath, every inch of him fighting for control.

"Julia didn't mean to upset you," Mary continued. "Neither did I. She was excited to show me. She...she wants to know who her mother was."

"Gone," Simon said, his throat tight. "She's gone. That's all she needs to know."

They sat there quietly. Suddenly, he glanced down as Mary's hand touched his briefly, then put it back in her lap.

"I can't imagine the pain you feel having lost the woman you love," Mary said. "And I know I'm a stranger, and your past is none of my business, but I don't think you know the pain Julia feels. By hiding your wife, her mother, away in your heart you might think you are preserving her.

"But you aren't. You aren't keeping her alive. I have learned this myself. You will lose your wife's memories as time passes. It's a horrible thing to admit, but it's true. I don't even remember my parents. But if you will share her stories and about who she was, Julia will keep her alive. As will her children one day. Then she will still be with you. All of you."

His throat bobbed. She spoke the truth, even if he hadn't wanted to hear it. But what right had she? She was correct in that it was none of her business. None whatsoever.

Simon reached into his mind, closing his eyes and trying to recall his wife's face. It was fuzzy. Which was why he had the photographs. Why he was so desperate not to have anything happen to them, because if it did, then he couldn't remember her.

The fingers of his hand curled into a fist. He didn't want that. Didn't want to forget about her. But he couldn't share her with anyone. It would hurt too much to remember, to speak of her.

"Is this why you have been so resistant to the idea of a governess?" Mary asked. "You are worried more of your wife will slip away? That Julia will love that woman more?"

This woman and her incessant questions! He glanced at her, and saw something in her eyes that pierced him. It wasn't pity. He was glad; he couldn't have handled that. No, it was...understanding? It deflated his anger.

"I don't know," he said quietly. "Maybe."

She nodded. "I understand. I've...I've never had anything so precious to hold on to, but I am sure I might feel the same." She stood then, and started toward the attic stairs. "I'm going to check on Julia, so she knows you aren't angry with her. Just...perhaps think about what I've said. Maybe the two of you can figure out a way to keep the memory of her mother alive. I don't think your daughter will ever want to replace her. She's desperate to know who she was."

"Meghan," Simon said softly. "Her name was Meghan."

There was silence, and then he heard Mary leave, her shoes fading on the wooden stairs.

Opening the trunk once more, he took out one of the photographs, and stared at it until his eyes blurred so completely from the tears he couldn't see anything at all.

Chapter 13

Mary carefully went down the attic stairs, trying not to tremble and drop the lantern she held. She was also trying very hard—though quite unsuccessfully—not to worry that she'd just gotten herself fired, before she'd even had a chance to prove she could be a governess, and earn some much needed money.

What had she been thinking, telling Simon such a thing? She should know better, having been in service for years. You never, ever questioned your employer nor shared your own opinions on something. Here she'd done exactly that. And worst of all, about a sensitive subject. The loss of his wife!

Mary stepped into the hallway and went to Julia's door. Would her presence be welcome, or would it be better if she left her alone? Mary bit her lip while she hesitated, her gaze flickering between Julia's room and the attic door.

"Is that you, Mary?" Julia asked.

"Yes, I'm right here," Mary answered, coming closer. She walked in, and realized the girl was lying on her bed facedown and sniffling.

"Are you all right?" Mary asked softly, resting her arm on Julia's back.

Julia turned over. "Papa is sure to be angry with me. That's why I didn't want him to know. I just...I just wanted to show you those special things."

"They are special indeed," Mary agreed. "I was glad to see the picture of your mother. You look a great deal alike. Both very beautiful."

The shy but pleased smile Julia gave her warmed Mary. She wished she could say more to comfort the girl. Truthfully, she needed comfort as well. She wasn't sure if Simon meant for her to leave the house. She'd have to wait for him to come downstairs to ask, but she had the feeling that she'd be on the stage at the soonest possibility.

It was better that way. She'd have to leave eventually, even if she didn't quite know where to go, especially if Cal might run across her. She didn't want that. Mary simply wanted to start over. Have a life of her own making, since it was now painfully obvious she couldn't be part of anyone else's.

Not for the first time since she'd arrived, Mary wished she'd never come. She'd have saved herself so much heartache. She stilled then. In some small way, she and Simon were similar. Sparing himself heartache was what he was trying to do. And could she blame him?

While she'd lost out on a future with Cal—though perhaps she was spared—and she found herself with little means and a great deal of uncertainty ahead of her, Simon had lost the person he'd devoted his life to, had loved, and had brought a child into the world with.

She couldn't blame him for wanting to forget the pain that came with all of that. To hold on tightly to the things he had of his wife's, to cling to his daughter.

While she hadn't been wrong in what she'd said, it wasn't her place, and Mary regretted having opened her mouth. She should have just left. But something in his face...the way he'd looked so lost. It had called to her. That feeling his expression gave her was a familiar one. She felt it too, even if she hadn't gone through as much as he had.

"Do you think Papa will be upset at me forever?" Julia asked, startling Mary. She'd been so caught up in her own thoughts, she forgot she was there in the little girl's room, trying to make her feel better.

"How could anyone be upset with you?" Mary asked lightly. She helped Julia to sit up, and offered her a handkerchief. "I think this was just one of the times that you had questions. You have so many, I am sure he will realize this is just another one of them. However, thinking about and talking about your mother makes your father sad. He misses her a good deal."

"I know," Julia said, twisting the tiny piece of fabric between her fingers. "He doesn't ever smile. Or laugh. Not really. Mrs. Thomas calls it not meeting his eyes, whatever that means. What does that mean?"

Mary thought carefully. "I think she must mean that he is a little happy when he smiles or laughs, but can't quite find his way through the sadness fully in order to give a big smile or laugh. The kind that makes your cheeks or stomach hurt, and you all breathless with giggles."

She poked Julia's stomach. "Just like the kind we had over that silly joke you told about the fish."

Julia giggled, and her sweet smile made Mary feel slightly relieved that she'd helped her feel better. At least a little.

"It's a complicated thing, being a grownup," Mary continued. "So, enjoy your childhood as much as you can."

"That's what Mrs. Thomas says too," Julia said, crinkling her nose. "But I think it will be great fun to be grown up and do whatever I want to do."

"I hope you get just that," Mary said. "Now, there's still a great deal we can do today. It won't be dinner for quite some time. What would you like to do? Should we work on making a new dress for one of your dolls? Mrs. Thomas said she had some fabric scraps we could dig through. I bet we can find something lovely."

"I guess so," Julia said, still looking in her lap. "It's just..."

"What, my dear?" Mary asked, wrapping an arm around her shoulders.

"It's just Papa is sure to tell me I can never go up there again. So, how will I know about my mother now?"

Mary wasn't sure how to answer. She nearly worked her mind into a frenzy, trying to think what she could say to give the girl a satisfactory answer, when she heard the clearing of a throat.

Simon stood in the doorway, a framed photograph in his hand. "I'll tell you about her," he said, walking inside.

There was a gasp, and Julia gaped at her father. Sensing this was a moment just for the two of them, Mary quickly slipped out of the room. Truthfully, she wanted to linger to learn more about the woman who'd not only stolen Simon's heart, but had kept it captured years after her death.

What would it be like to have a love such as that? She'd never know. There wouldn't be anything so wonderful for her.

Mary returned to her room, wiping the tears from her eyes. Before Cal, there had been no one. Now that he'd left her, she was right where she'd started. Alone. It was foolish to think she'd ever have love the way others had.

Not her. Not ever.

Mary closed her bedroom door behind her and looked around. She didn't have much at all. Was this how her life was going to be? Always on the outside? Always in someone else's home, never her own?

Anger suddenly burned hotly in Mary. She was tempted to seek Cal out. Give him a piece of her mind. Demand that he pay for her stage ticket to leave. Why should she use the meager funds she had, when he could have sent her a letter telling her not to come? She could have still been working for Mrs. Miles, been figuring out a plan for her future.

Instead, she was here, out of pity, in the home of a man who was haunted by the losses he'd experienced, unknowing that they amplified both his daughter's, and her own.

It was too painful being here. She needed to leave.

Chapter 14

Simon's eyes felt swollen from the tears he'd shared with his daughter, as he'd talked to her about her mother, telling her stories and answering all the questions her little mind came up with. They'd talked nearly two hours, and it was getting late, nearly time for dinner.

Despite the heaviness he'd felt when he first walked into the room, he felt much lighter in his chest now, and it surprised him.

"I will leave this photograph with you," Simon said, placing it on the top of Julia's bookshelf, "and trust you to take good care of it."

"I will," Julia whispered, her eyes wide. "Oh, thank you, Papa!"

"I promise to always tell you whatever you want to know about your mother," he said. "I'm sorry it took me so long to be able to do so. But that's the past. Together, we will keep her memory alive."

Julia nodded, but she didn't answer, and when Simon looked, she had taken down a book with blank paper inside and had started to write in it. He tiptoed away so that he wouldn't interrupt whatever she was doing. He suspected she was trying to copy down the stories he'd told her. It was a very good idea, if she was, and made him wonder why he'd not attempted such a thing.

He realized why, then, the moment he thought it. It would have been too painful. But now that some of the rawness, the deep and terrible ache had eased a little, maybe he could do that for Julia.

However, he had something else important to do. Apologize to Mary.

Simon walked downstairs and peered into the sitting room. As he'd hoped, Mary was there, and appeared to be sewing doll clothes for Julia.

She glanced up when he walked in, an uncertain look on her face. Mary started to stand, and he said, "No, please don't let me interrupt."

Mary hesitated, then nodded. "I was making Julia a new dress for one of her dolls."

"You are very talented," Simon told her, taking in the tiny dress that was taking form under her fingers.

"Thank you. Before I came here, I often made doll clothing to sell. I always thought it would be fun to have a shop where I did that, and made matching dresses for girls."

"That's just the sort of thing Julia would love," he agreed.

She ventured, "Speaking of Julia, did...did your talk go well?"

"I think so." Simon sat down, and looked around the room thoughtfully. "It was...easier than I thought it would be, honestly." His eyes met hers. "Thank you for encouraging me to talk to her."

Mary's cheeks flushed. "I felt badly about what I said," she uttered, her voice low. "Please forgive me."

"It was only the truth," Simon said. "That's what I prefer, so there is nothing to forgive. But I do owe you an apology."

"Me? Why?" Mary asked.

"Because I think you were right. I've known it all along, but hearing someone say something and then actually admitting it beyond your own self is a difficult thing. I thought I was protecting Julia from pain, and, yes, from someone replacing her mother. But after you went downstairs, and I was alone in the attic, I remembered something Meghan had said often."

"What is that?" Mary asked.

"The heart is like an ocean. There's room enough for everyone. I had forgotten that." He studied Mary. She was still sewing, quietly, but he didn't miss the faint tremble in her lip. "I shouldn't have thought or worried that you or anyone else was trying to replace Meghan. You aren't. There's room in Julia's heart for many people."

Suddenly, she said, "When you said to go, I wanted you to know, I will. I can. May I wait until morning, though?"

"No," Simon said, shaking his head. Then he saw the terror on her face as her head shot up and her eyes met his. "What I meant," he quickly said, "was no, I don't want you to go. I want you to stay. You are good for Julia. Good for...me."

The last was said so quietly, he wasn't sure she'd heard it. But then a small flush spread over her cheeks.

"I have something unpleasant I must tell you, though," Simon said, leaning forward and lacing his fingers. "I hate to change the subject, but this is very important."

She frowned slightly, the needle pausing in the fabric. "I'm listening."

"Today at the bank, a man came in by the name of Cal Lynch. He wanted a loan."

A whole gamut of emotions flew across Mary's face. He wasn't sure which upset him the most. The fear, great by the way her hands stilled and she began to pluck at the fabric she held, or the hurt, that started in her eyes and made her lip quiver again. For some reason he couldn't explain, he wanted to protect her from what she was feeling. Comfort her.

It wouldn't have been proper, though, so he stayed still, squeezing the arm of the chair to keep himself from reaching toward her.

"Is...is that so?" she finally asked.

"Yes, I wanted to warn you. I don't intend to loan him anything. I understand he has quite a few debts, however, he told me that he could get you to vouch for his repayments. And he..." Simon wasn't sure he could finish, not with the look of horror on Mary's face, but he knew he had to.

"He knows you've not left town, and he'd said that he intended to either ask for the money you promised him in trade for him leaving you alone, or enter into a relationship with you again. Until he had the money. He seems to think that it belongs to him because you were bringing it here to him."

Mary drew in a sharp breath. "He would," she said. "I'm sure of it. No one ever told Cal no to anything. No matter that he didn't earn it, and I did, and it was for our future." She closed her eyes for a moment and shook her head. "I can't, though. I can't just give him what I have. There's no guarantee that he would leave me be. And I...I am on my own now. I need to provide for myself."

He was about to tell her that he'd see she was cared for, but would she take it the wrong way? He wasn't sure. He also wasn't sure just how he meant it. Or how he could keep her safe.

"I promise not to let him know you are here," Simon told her.

"But he still may find out," she said softly, finishing the thought in his mind.

The bell rang for dinner, and Mary put the doll's dress into her sewing basket. Simon stood and smiled at Julia, who had just bounded down the stairs. He tried not to let Mary's distressed face draw his eyes. He might not be able to look away.

Julia chattered away on the walk to the table and told them a joke about a fish, which set them all to laughing. Mary's shoulders seemed to ease from the tension she'd been wearing. That relieved Simon as well.

As they ate dinner together, with Mrs. Thomas's thick noodles smothered in gravy, Simon couldn't help but notice how different everything felt. Brighter. Lighter. It was as though his tears had cleaned him, restored him.

Except his burdens seemed to now be on Mary. Her shoulders were tense once more, and he knew that she was likely very worried about what he'd told her. He'd have to let her know she wasn't needing to face Cal on her own, that he'd be there to send the man away if necessary. At the first moment alone, he would.

After dinner, Julia curled next to him with a book, and Simon read the newspaper. Mary was sitting nearby, having resumed working on the doll's dress. Julia had gotten up to look at it several times, and had begged Mary to make her more. Mary had laughed, and humored her, agreeing to dig through the scrap bag again soon. Simon planned to ask Mary if he could pay her extra, to surprise Julia with several dresses and matching doll dresses.

A strange feeling crept over Simon just then as he glanced about the content room. Was this what it would have been like, if Meghan were here?

Just as quickly, he thought no. It wouldn't. Meghan detested sewing. She'd have been reading, like he'd seen Mary do. Or out in the garden, also like Mary seemed to enjoy. His eyes took in Mary, her intense focus on each stitch, the care she was giving to the doll's dress, but also the way she'd stop, on occasion, and her shoulders would sink down slightly.

The urge to comfort her returned. As soon as he realized that, he shook his head, telling himself it was simply that he was grateful for her, that she'd caused him to release some of the hurt he'd felt, and he wanted to repay the kindness. That was all. That was the only reason everything made him think of her.

But was it?

Maybe there was more. Maybe he liked her being around. He was lonely. Did miss the companionship of a woman.

And Mary—was not interested in someone like him. A man who kept yelling at her. Who, hours before, had been crying over his long deceased wife.

But if there ever would be room for someone new in his heart, he had the feeling she'd be a good fit.

The clock on the wall chimed, startling him, and Simon stood. "Time for you to go to bed," he told Julia.

She didn't pout, just nodded and put her book on the shelf.

"How about a bedtime story?" Mary asked, following his daughter up the stairs.

A half hour later, Simon left his study and stopped suddenly, as he bumped into someone.

"Goodness," Mary gasped, watching as the tea in her cup splashed about the brim.

"Forgive me," he said. "I was about to look for you."

He watched as she nodded, that uncertain look filling her eyes once more. A wave of sympathy flooded him. What had she been like before Cal had hurt her? Had she been a confident woman? He thought she might be. He could see glimpses of it, had, in fact, when she'd spoken with him in the attic.

So, what was it that made her worried all of a sudden? He wondered if she might think he was about to tell her he had changed his mind about allowing her a trial period.

"Here I am," she answered, giving him a small smile, though her voice was slightly strained. "How can I help you?"

"I wanted to apologize for my anger and my abruptness once more," he said. "I'm not usually that way. It wasn't until this afternoon I realized I hadn't let myself grieve her. Not until now. For some reason, much of the hurt and anger that had been filling me fled."

"It's completely understandable, considering the situation," Mary hastened to assure him. "Think nothing of it."

He nodded, but looked past her, a small frown on his face. When he looked at her again, he said, "When I lost my wife, Julia's mother, everything in my life had one purpose, and that was to protect our daughter."

Mary said, "I understand. I had the feeling that was the case." She bit her lip, and softly said, "I assure you, I'd never let harm come to her."

"I realize that," he said. "It's just...harm can come in many forms. Which is why I try to be careful in all ways, with what we talk about. For example, her mother. That's why I'd avoided the subject. But now...well, I have told Julia I will answer any questions she has, but I still prefer she not go into the attic. Her mother's wedding dress is up there, and one day...maybe one day Julia will want to wear it. So I'd like to keep it in good condition."

The smile Mary gave him was brilliant. "I think that's a wonderful idea," she told him. "I imagine it made Julia so happy to hear."

"It did," he said with a small chuckle. "There's one more thing," he added. When she looked at him expectantly, he said, "I don't want you to worry about Cal. If he bothers you, come to me. I'll take care of him."

She gave him a strange look, then asked, almost as though she didn't quite believe him, "You would?"

"Yes. I don't want you to feel concerned for your safety."

There. That was safe. Not quite what he'd wanted to say, but he'd managed to sound professional and concerned. But, for some reason he couldn't explain, he felt incredibly nervous. "That's all," Simon said. "I didn't mean to keep you."

"Not at all," Mary said. "Thank you. I appreciate your concern."

"Goodnight then," he said, stepping to the side.

Mary moved past, but her foot caught on the corner of the rug. As she lurched forward, his hand wrapped around her waist, the other behind her back.

Before Simon realized he'd even attempted to catch her, Mary was in his arms.

Chapter 15

To her surprise, not a drop of the tea splashed outside of the cup where it waved, dangerously close to spilling over.

She looked down at the arm around her, and then nearly ached at the loss as it pulled away and she was released. It had felt so...nice. As though it fit perfectly. Her heart started to pound, her middle tingled, and Mary looked anywhere but at Simon. "Thank you," she said. "I'm terribly clumsy."

He cleared his throat. "Not at all. I've tripped there myself several times."

She shot a quick glance toward him, but couldn't tell from his flushed expression what he might be thinking. Quickly, he walked toward the kitchen. "Goodnight," he said.

"Goodnight," Mary echoed.

She returned to her room, where she drank her tea, and then lay in bed, wide awake. What had just happened? That feeling in her? She'd never felt anything like that before, not even with Cal.

"What does it mean?" Mary whispered.

But she knew the answer, without even thinking more about it. It meant nothing. Because Simon had no interest in any woman filling the void his wife had left in any capacity. Not with a new wife, not with a governess, and not with any female at all. Especially her. And she shouldn't even be thinking such a thing! Hadn't the man just been grieving his wife tonight?

But for some reason she couldn't explain, that made the ache in her heart feel worse. Mary wiped at the hot tear that suddenly rolled down her cheek. It reminded her of her recent loss. She'd never be wanted, would she? No one had wanted her before Cal. He had easily replaced her, and now...now, she found herself in the home of a man who she was, terrifyingly so, feeling attracted to. With, once again, no hope of affection returned.

Simon had offered her protection if Cal bothered her. But did he mean it? What would he do if Cal did come around? Find her? Demand her money? Perhaps most importantly, what would she do? If she thought for a moment he would go away and never bother her again, she'd likely give her hard earned dollars.

But any man who lied the way he had, to the woman he claimed to love, would be lying again. She couldn't trust him.

Mary tried to stop her thoughts from the long spiral she knew they were headed for, and the restless night that she was sure to have. But she wasn't able to. Each time she closed her eyes, she felt Simon's arms around her, and wondered what it would be like to feel them again.

The next morning, she felt exhausted, but dressed quickly, helped Julia down for breakfast, and then ate before returning to her room to get ready for the Sunday morning service.

The four of them walked to the church in town, and Mary wouldn't have been afraid or embarrassed to admit that she was concerned Cal might be there. Then she realized that was quite unlikely. Cal was not the sort to go to church. He'd always refused when she invited him. Though the memory only slightly relaxed her, Mary hoped it would allow her to keep her attention on the reverend, and not let her eyes wander around.

Mrs. Thomas sat herself on one end of the pew, and Julia promptly sat next to her. That left Mary to sit next to Simon. Throughout the sermon, she nearly held her breath, almost terrified to be so close to him. When she breathed in deeply, she could smell his shaving soap, so fresh, so delightful, and just a little spicy.

And now and again, when she found her thoughts roaming in that completely inappropriate way, she'd pinch herself, trying to keep her thoughts on the reason they were there in the first place.

She also scolded herself. She hardly knew Simon. In fact, she wasn't completely sure he still wanted her there. He might, as he'd done before, lose his temper. Send her away, even if he'd apologized and said that wasn't usually like him.

What was he usually like? Or, what had he been like before the loss of his wife? Was he a man who laughed at everything? Brooded? Was he helpful and kind and caring?

And why was she becoming so attached to the man and unable to stop thinking about him? Was it because when she did, she felt happy? And when she thought of Cal, she felt hurt and betrayed?

"Our paths often seem long," the reverend said, from where he stood in front of those listening. "Winding. Uncertain."

That was for certain. Her path had been anything but what she'd expected from the time she arrived.

"There will be many times, you'll be walking along and wonder how you found yourself where you are. Did you get turned around? Did the road you were on lead to a forest with bears and darkness, not the field of wheat you'd thought you were walking to?" The reverend stood before them, meeting every eye.

Mary felt as though he were talking directly to her. Yes, that had indeed happened.

"Have you wondered even now, how you are to find your way? What awaits you on the other side of the dark forest?"

"Yes," Mary whispered. "I have."

"What was that?" Simon asked, leaning in closely.

Mary was so distracted, she missed what the reverend said next. "Oh, er, I didn't mean to speak," she whispered.

If he was going to say something, it was lost in the noise as the churchgoers rose to their feet, and sang the closing hymn. She'd have to ask Mrs. Thomas to tell her what was said. After a final prayer, everyone shuffled forward to the large church doors, where the reverend stood, shaking hands as each person departed.

"Excellent sermon," Simon said, as they approached. "It's good to see you."

Mary said the same, and was glad that as the man started to ask who she was, someone else came along behind her, and started asking questions of the reverend. She wasn't sure why she didn't want to linger and speak to others. There was no shame in being a governess, but that wasn't how she wanted to introduce herself.

And, she also didn't want more people than necessary to know that she was Cal Lynch's former intended. She was still anxious about being in the open on the street, concerned he might find her.

Simon stood talking with a few people about a dozen paces away, and Mary couldn't help but take the opportunity to observe him. He seemed different today. Not just because he was at church and acting like a better version of himself, like some people did, but he just...seemed different. She couldn't place why she thought that.

As he smiled and nodded, several men, and a few obviously unmarried women, stopped by. Mary couldn't help but feel a little restless at that sight.

"He seems more like his old self, with some of his grief lifted," Mrs. Thomas said, coming to stand next to her. "Julia told me what happened. I think you are responsible for this change."

"Me? Oh no," Mary stammered. "But I'm glad for it, and glad that he and Julia now won't keep her mother's memories locked away."

"It makes me happy to see him returning to his old self," the housekeeper said. "Don't discount what I said, though. I have tried to speak with him through the years, but nothing happened until you did."

"Did you know him before you started to work for him?" Mary asked. "I thought you came on when Julia was born."

"Yes, but I was with him for a short time before she was born. Enough time to see that he was a young man filled with happiness and love." Mrs. Thomas looked fondly at him. "This is a good step in the right direction."

"What do you mean?" Mary asked, falling into step as they walked toward him and Julia.

"I mean that you young people, sometimes when a tragedy strikes, you withdraw. You shrink into yourselves. Think that's the end, that there's nothing more in life for you. That's not always the case." She paused and raised an eyebrow at Mary. "That's not the case for him, and that's certainly not the case for you."

Mary's eyes widened, and she stammered, "I-I..."

The housekeeper just patted her hand, and then said louder as she walked toward Simon, "Thank you for waiting for me, Mr. Alexander. I found my handbag right in our pew."

"No trouble at all," Simon said, and turned, walking toward home. "I'm glad you retrieved it, instead of remembering once we had gotten most of the way home."

"That makes two of us," the housekeeper agreed with a laugh.

Mary walked next to Julia, but her attention was on anything but the girl. A woman with blonde curls, big blue eyes, and a complexion that could only be considered flawless waved, and called, "Yoohoo! Mr. Alexander!"

Stopping, Simon glanced around, and then smiled, nodding his head. "Miss Marlin," he said.

"Who is that?" Mary whispered.

"One of Mr. Alexander's acquaintance's daughters," Mrs. Thomas said, though her lips were pressed into a line. "I know it isn't right, but something about her sets my hackles up. It appears that we aren't the only ones to notice the weights lifted off of Mr. Alexander's shoulders."

"I agree," Mary said, then covered her mouth as she realized she'd spoken out loud. She, Julia, and Mrs. Thomas set out at a slow pace, while Simon and the woman talked for a few moments alone.

When Mary glanced quickly over her shoulder, she saw the woman laughing, her hand on his arm, and standing quite close to him. Her chest squeezed. Which was quite silly. He was her employer, nothing more. She had no right at all to feel jealous.

Mary wished she could see Simon's face, but his back was to her. All she could see was Miss Marlin smiling up at him, far too close for her liking.

But when Simon caught up a few moments later, humming under his breath, Mary couldn't help but feel envy in her every pore. Now that he was starting to come out from the cloud of blackness that had traveled over him, was Miss Marlin about to become Mrs. Alexander?

And was that all her fault?

Chapter 16

It wasn't that Mrs. Thomas wasn't a fine cook every day of the week, but Simon always enjoyed the Sunday meals especially. In addition to the fried chicken, biscuits, corn, and fried potatoes, she'd made a strawberry cobbler today, and he'd had two helpings.

He'd had to. Cobbler didn't keep. Or so she'd insisted, and he wasn't about to argue.

The day had passed quickly, for as slow as Sundays seemed to go. Simon wandered from the dining room to his study, looking for the book he'd been reading. He hoped to get a few chapters read before he got too tired and went to bed.

Though he wasn't ready to admit it, having Mary there to help with Julia had actually relieved some of his stress, not added to it. He didn't feel as though Julia's full care landed on his shoulders, and he knew when he'd have to travel, that there would be a second person there to help care for her, if it was needed. After all, it wasn't right to let Mrs. Thomas take care of everything around the house all of the time.

There was a soft tap at his door, and Simon called, "Come in."

The door pushed open slowly, and his gaze fell on Julia, who stood, waiting. "You can come in," Simon said, wondering why she appeared hesitant.

She entered, pushing the door behind her and walked over, standing in front of his desk with the serious expression on her face she usually reserved for her most difficult questions.

Simon steeled himself. The last time she'd looked like this, she'd wanted to know when he'd give her a little brother or sister, and he'd had a very...uncomfortable discussion.

"Papa," Julia finally said, sitting in the chair across from him, "I have a question."

"I wondered if you might," Simon said. He laced his fingers together and placed them on top of his desk. "I'm ready."

"I saw you at church today," Julia said.

"Did you? I saw you too," Simon teased.

His joke had the intended result, and Julia laughed. "Yes, Papa! I was there with you."

"Did something else catch your attention?" Simon asked.

"No, but Miss Marlin sure was trying to catch yours," Julia said, in a voice that sounded a great deal like Mrs. Thomas's. He wondered if that's where she'd gotten her question. Had the housekeeper been talking to someone and Julia overheard? But before he was able to say anything, she continued, "If you are going to remarry, and get me a new mother, can I please have Mary instead? I like her much better than any of the women you were talking to."

Simon's mouth fell open. This...this was not at all what he'd expected his daughter to say. "I...well, I..."

"It's okay, Papa. You don't have to ask her right this moment," Julia said, sliding up from her chair. "I understand these things take time to arrange."

"It's not that simple," Simon finally managed. How was it his daughter sounded so grown up, for such a young age? He gave a small frown. "I'm not sure how to explain to you that I'm not ready to get married yet. I might not ever marry again."

Julia paused, tipped her head, and asked, "Why?"

How he hated that follow-up word sometimes.

"Because," Simon finally said, "I am not looking for a wife."

"Why?"

He winced. "Because I am quite content with things the way they are right now. We have Mrs. Thomas, and we have Mary."

"But if you married Mary, then she wouldn't leave once she figured out where she was going to go," Julia said, her tone one of practicality. "Unless you do, we might not get to have Mary. I don't want my days to be without her. Do you know she might open her own little shop and sew dresses for girls like me?"

"Yes, but one doesn't marry simply to be convenient for all involved," Simon reminded his daughter, though he was aware such things had happened. "There must be love involved. At least, there should be."

"*I* love Mary," Julia said.

"I know you do." He sighed. "Why is it I have the feeling that no matter what I might say today, it won't be quite the answer that you are looking for?"

Julia nodded slowly, with a thoughtful expression on her face. She placed her hand on the door's knob. "I think you are right. It won't be. But it might be different tomorrow. I'll ask then."

She left then, nearly skipping out of the study, and Simon just stared at the closed door, shaking his head slightly and chuckling. To be a child again, where everything was simple. Right, wrong. Up, down. Easy, complicated.

Once you were older, trying to figure out your place beyond your parents' home, things were much more difficult. Something Julia had said just then replayed in his mind. Mary. That's right, she wasn't here permanently. She was on a trial basis. One that both of them may no longer want. Though he was getting more comfortable with her there, even enjoyed the idea, it was apparent she was still planning for her future.

Why should she not? She needed to. Unless…he tapped a finger on the desk. Unless he made her realize that she was welcome, could have a job here. That might make Mary feel more secure about her future. It would also let him see Mary as often as—

This wasn't about him. Not at all. So, where had that thought started to creep up from?

Simon pressed a hand to his heart. Why was it pounding so frantically? Stress. It must have been stress.

He dropped his head into his hands, feeling the weight of his elbows on the hard wood of his desk. He honestly hadn't cared for Miss Marlin coming up to him today. Though he had been friends with her father for years, he'd never had a high opinion of the young woman.

Almost a dozen years his junior, he'd watched her grow from a spoiled child to a woman just the same. It was obvious that she'd also never be the kind of a mother that Julia would need. In fact, he wasn't sure Miss Marlin had ever even said hello to Julia.

Meanwhile, Mary, an absolute stranger, had connected to his daughter in such a way that Simon had no doubt she'd make an excellent—governess. Just governess.

With a groan, he stood. Too hard. Things were too hard just now. He headed out of his study, deciding bed was what he needed. A reprieve from his endless thoughts. But just as he exited, he smacked right into someone.

Mary.

"Forgive me," he said instantly, his hands reaching out to steady her. Small zaps of something shot through his hands, and he reluctantly pulled them away.

"My goodness. I really need to watch where I'm walking. Two days in a row! I'm sorry," Mary said, her cheeks flaming red.

"It's completely my fault," Simon assured her. She gave him a small smile and nod, then turned to walk away, when he asked, "Mary, have you a moment?"

"Yes, of course," she said.

"I realize we've not completely settled the matter of if you want to stay on as governess," he said. "Julia adores you, and I think it is only a matter of time before she's demanding an answer."

"No, we have not," Mary answered. "I admit, I wasn't sure you wanted me."

"I didn't, at first, but that's changed. I hope you know that. You've not been here long, but you seem to fit in perfectly. Fill a spot that we didn't realize needed filling."

She blinked at him several times. "That might be one of the kindest things anyone's ever said to me." Then she bit her lip. "I'd like to stay..."

"But?" he prompted.

She let out a small sigh. "This wasn't the future I'd planned for myself. And a small part of it is here, in town, potentially going to threaten me for my money. I don't know if it's wise for me to stay, for myself and for any of you, yet I have not had a chance to learn where would be best to go."

"I won't let him harass you," Simon said. "I promise you that."

"It's kind of you, but also not your responsibility," Mary said. "In truth, I still am unsure which would be better to do. Leaving town is the practical thing, but..." A wistful look came over her face.

"What?" Simon asked softly.

"I would miss Julia so very much. It sounds silly, I know, but I feel so very connected to her. May I have just a few days to think about it? I don't want to hurt Julia, but it may be unavoidable. I will be finished with the first set of dresses you'd requested I make. However, if I do leave, I will promise to write her often, with your permission. I blame Cal for all of this, and I don't want to fear for my safety, nor put you or Julia or Mrs. Thomas, who has been so kind to me, in a compromising position."

"I understand," Simon said. "Julia would miss you greatly as well. Of course, you could write. But don't let her be the reason you stay or leave. You need to do what's best for you."

"Thank you," Mary said, leaving quickly before he could say anything else.

He watched her walk away, not missing the slight droop of her shoulders. If he looked in the mirror, would he see the same in his?

He'd meant every word about her fitting in so well. He'd also meant what he'd said about keeping her safe from Cal, if it came down to it. But how could he ever tell her the whisper that had been floating around in his mind? That he didn't want her to leave because he would miss her? That, though she'd only been here a short time, like Julia, he couldn't imagine his days without Mary.

What did all of that mean?

No, he knew what it meant.

But was he ready to let himself even consider the idea of opening his heart to someone new?

Chapter 17

"Are you sure it's no bother?" Mrs. Thomas asked.

"Not at all," Mary assured her. "Let me have your shopping list and I'll take care of it. You, however, are to take care of that ankle of yours. It won't heal if you don't stay off it."

"Of all the bad luck," Mrs. Thomas sighed, glancing down at her swollen foot. "I walk up and down these stairs a dozen times a day! How in the world did I miss the last step?"

"It happens to everyone at some point. I've done the same. Now, can I get you anything before I go?" Mary asked.

"I'm drawing you a picture, Mrs. Thomas," Julia said, her face one of concentration.

"Thank you, Julia," Mrs. Thomas said. "You will be good company for me while Mary is gone. But, no, Mary, I don't need anything else. I appreciate it, though."

Mary nodded. "I'll fetch you paper and a pencil, and while you work on the list, I'll get myself ready. No worrying about meals, either. I'm quite capable of cooking."

"I'm so glad you are here," the housekeeper said.

"Three days," Simon said, walking into the sitting room and putting his hands on his hips. "That's what Doctor Jones said. Think you can keep off of it that long?"

Mrs. Thomas pressed her lips together. "It will be hard," she finally admitted. "I am not used to being still."

Mary brought her the paper. "The days will pass quickly. In the meantime, you enjoy your break. You aren't useless, though," she said with a wink. "If you get bored, I'll set you to shelling peas or peeling potatoes!"

"Good," Mrs. Thomas declared.

"Are you going into town now?" Simon asked, as he followed Mary into the foyer.

"Yes. I thought I would. Unless you need me to do something else?" Mary asked.

"I'll go with you, if you'd like," Simon said. "Company, someone to carry and..."

He didn't finish, but Mary had the feeling she knew just what he was thinking. Cal. Just in case Cal was there.

"I'd be grateful," Mary told him. "I just need a minute before we leave."

Simon nodded, and Mary hurried upstairs to her room. She took a moment to smooth down her hair. For a half second, she thought about changing her dress, but that would be silly. Simon didn't care what she wore. She was hired help. Nothing more.

She grabbed her handbag and headed down the stairs, then got the two large baskets that Mrs. Thomas used when she went shopping. As she walked into the sitting room, the housekeeper was just finishing the list and offered it to her.

"Mind you check he doesn't short me on the tea," Mrs. Thomas said with a sniff. "Sometimes I suspect his thumb is on the scale."

"I'll watch closely," Mary promised, dropping the list into one of the baskets. She put one in each arm and walked outside to the front porch where Simon waited.

"Here, I can carry one," he offered, taking a basket.

They walked along quietly, but it didn't feel uncomfortable. Mary wasn't sure what she'd have done if it did. "Thank you for going with me," she finally said.

"I'm happy to." Simon looked up at the sky. "It's a nice day for it."

"Yes. I'm hoping it stays that way." Mary's eyes traveled along the area. The houses spread out, the beaten prairie path, the small town off in the distance.

"Can I ask you something?" Simon said suddenly. "It's personal, so feel free to say no."

"Let me hear it first," Mary said. "Then I'll see if I want to answer."

"That's fair. I've been wondering, what in the world did you see in that Cal fellow?" Simon asked.

She laughed. "That's a good question! It's one I've asked myself at least a hundred times in the last few days."

"Have you figured it out?" Simon asked.

"Not yet. Believe it or not, the man I saw when I got here wasn't the one I'd pledged myself to." Mary's chest squeezed slightly at the memory of that day. "When Cal and I first met, it wasn't love at first sight. It was just hello. And I don't quite know how it happened, that eventually we saw more and more of each other, but I do know that I felt proud when he asked me to marry him, and very excited to be heading west. To make our own life, build up our own land, and have something worth protecting."

"I think most all of us want that in life. That thing that's worth fighting for," Simon mused.

"Yes. I think so too." Mary shook her head. "There were no warning signs, not really. But it's likely there would have been, had I been around Simon more. However, when you are a housemaid, with only Sundays off, and then just a half day every other week, you don't get to get out much and spend time with others, let alone your intended. It's very easy to deceive someone if you only see them a few hours once a week. And that's all we did. Sunday afternoons."

"I'm sorry," Simon said, meeting her eyes. "None of this has been fair to you. I...I admire how well you are recovering, though."

"That's only because I have no choice," Mary said softly. "What else can I do? I've got to take care of myself."

"Not by yourself," Simon said. "I'm here too, if you need me."

She gave him a small smile, but it was tinged with sadness. In what way did he mean that? Only one of friendliness, she was sure.

They walked in silence for a moment. "I must be honest," Mary said suddenly. "I envy you."

"Me?"

"Yes." She frowned slightly. "I hope this doesn't come out the wrong way. Sometimes, things make sense inside of my head, but make a terrible confused jumble when they get out."

"Try. I'll keep that in mind," he promised.

"I envy you having had love. The kind that lasts, that never fades. That meant you were worth loving, and valued, and treasured. I hate that you suffer for it, but I think that it would be wonderful to know just what it feels like. Even if it's snatched away."

Was her voice starting to wobble? The tingling in her eyes and nose led her to believe so. Mary quickly stopped talking. She was determined not to let what happened with Cal stay with her and cause her pain.

"Is Cal your first love?" Simon asked, his voice gentle.

"My first, and only," Mary said. "At my age, it's very unlikely I'll have another chance. Even if I move away. The only option I see for marriage is to become a mail-order bride, and I admit I'm not sure I am brave enough for that idea."

"It's not a good idea," Simon agreed hastily. "And I hope you won't consider it. But there's something else I want to tell you."

"What is that?" Mary asked.

"Cal is a fool. He should never have betrayed your heart or your trust. I think he's going to regret that, if he doesn't already." Simon scowled, as if he could see Cal. Just to be sure, Mary glanced around quickly, hoping he wasn't nearby.

He wasn't.

Her shoulders relaxed.

"I'm sure he does, if he needs my money," Mary said lightly, though she felt anything but. It was strange, discussing her lack of love or a future with Simon.

"I mean, he'll regret losing you," Simon said. "One day, he'll wake up, realize that he had a good thing, and he threw it away. I wouldn't have."

Mary stilled and stared at him. As if he just then realized what he'd said, Simon stammered, "I mean, you see—"

"I understand," Mary said quickly, catching up to him, though she honestly didn't.

She let the words play around in her mind for a few moments. How nice it would be to have someone think such things about her. To value her as much as she did them. To want to love, and protect, and make happy the other.

"I've got to put a letter into the safe at the bank," Simon said. "Will you be fine for a few moments in the store?"

"Of course," Mary said. She waved her hand at him. "Go ahead."

He nodded and crossed the street to the bank. Mary pushed open the general store door. Her eyes slid across the new display of fabrics before her. A purple one, as soft as the buds on a newly forming iris beckoned her, and she reached toward it.

And then froze as she heard her name.

"Mary Clinton, there you are. I've been hoping to see you."

She sucked in a breath. She didn't have to turn or even look over to see who it was. "Cal."

"I think we should talk," he told her, stepping closer. "We've so much to discuss."

"There's nothing more for either of us to say," Mary answered firmly, stepping to the side.

"Oh, there is," Cal said, blocking her path, a sneer on his face. "A whole lot more."

Chapter 18

Simon unlocked the safe, glad to be alone where no one could see him. He couldn't believe he'd said what he had. How he'd almost confessed that he cared for her. Did he care for her? He thought so, even though he hadn't known her long. It had been like that with Meghan too. They hadn't been acquainted but for a few weeks when they just knew.

Could it be he was going to get a second chance at love? Not just that, but the opportunity to be someone else's second chance at love? The idea was scary. Filled with worry, mixed with just the smallest bit of wonder at the idea.

But he wasn't ready for that yet. Wasn't sure that he could ever fully allow another into his heart, where once Meghan had captured it all.

Once he was sure the letter was secure, Simon locked the safe, and rose from the hard wooden floor. His gazed landed on the barred window in front of him, where Cal Lynch had stood on the opposite side, asking for a loan.

He still wondered what had possessed the man to ask for such a thing. He also wondered if Cal would return, asking again. It might be time to get a little help from the local sheriff. Perhaps he should have already spoken to him about all of this, but Mary hadn't seemed interested in doing so, and Cal hadn't done anything that affected him, yet, so he couldn't file a complaint.

Going to his desk, he scribbled a note, and then left the bank, checking the door twice to be sure it was locked, and headed next door to the sheriff's office.

When he went inside, the office was empty. That wasn't really a surprise. The sheriff and his deputy were likely over at the saloon, where he could hear a good deal of shouting. Simon set the note he'd written on the sheriff's desk and walked across to the general store.

As he walked in, he glanced around quickly looking for Mary. She looked pale, and appeared to be trembling.

"Are you well?" he asked, coming alongside her.

"Cal was here," she whispered. "He..." She stopped, and drew in a deep breath as her eyes darted to the other customers. "Let me get the items Mrs. Thomas needs."

Simon nodded. Of course. This wasn't the place to share such personal information, though he wondered if the shopkeeper had overheard what had happened.

Simon browsed around the store, keeping one eye on Mary. She seemed to be trying to distract herself with fabrics. He joined her and picked up a yellow print. "You would look nice with this one," he told her.

"It did catch my eye," she admitted. "But I was looking for Julia. She doesn't need anything, yet, but the way she's starting to grow, she'll need a few new dresses soon."

"Got your order ready," the store owner called.

"Thank you," Simon said, starting toward him. He paused and asked Mary, "Anything else?"

She shook her head.

Simon reached into his pocket for his money, then said, "Can you give me another jar of that tea? And a quarter's worth of peppermints, another of horehound, and three more pencils?"

"Sure can," the storekeeper said, adding those items to the basket. "That'll be seven dollars and twenty cents. Someone got a stomachache?"

"No, but Mrs. Thomas has turned her ankle, and I seem to recall she mentioned horehound helped a little with pains, stomachaches aside."

"That's what I hear too," the general owner said. "Send her my well wishes."

"I will," Simon said, then placed the money on the counter and picked up the baskets. As Mary reached for one, he said, "If you'll just get the door, I'll carry these."

"If you are sure?" she asked, walking over to the large door and opening it.

"Quite sure," he said, stepping outside into the sunshine and the cool breeze. The store had felt a little stuffy. He paused to readjust the baskets and continued toward the house. Though the baskets had been packed evenly, they were both a little more than he was sure Mary would be able to carry comfortably. Though he had no doubt she'd manage just fine, there was no need to, since he was there.

That was also why he always gave Mrs. Thomas the money to have Jim take her back home on her larger shopping days, so she didn't have to worry about carrying everything. When he wasn't available, she simply left it for him to deliver when he was.

Once they were a good distance away from anyone nearby, he wondered if Mary would tell him what had happened in the store during the short time he'd been away from her.

She didn't say anything, just seemed to look around everywhere but at him. He hesitated, but finally asked, "Tell me what happened with Cal."

He didn't miss the press of Mary's lips. "He was inside of the general store when I walked in," she explained. "He said we needed to talk."

Simon wanted to interrupt, to interject with a snort, or a question, but he let her continue.

"He..." She stopped talking, and Simon looked over with horror to see that Mary's face was starting to turn blotchy, and her lips were trembling.

"Let's stop a moment," he said, quickly leading her over to a few large trees, and setting the baskets down.

When they'd settled onto the grass, he offered his handkerchief. Mary took it, dabbing at her eyes.

"I'm sorry," she said.

"You've nothing to be sorry for," Simon assured her. "I do, however. I shouldn't have left you, not even for a moment."

"Luckily, our interaction wasn't too long," Mary said, closing her eyes for a moment. When she reopened them, he was struck by how her eyes were the most stunning shade of hazel. They locked on to his as she continued with her story.

"Cal was angry, at first. I think, however, he realized that wasn't the way to get anything out of me, or to make himself look good. He apologized, of course, and said he didn't know what he was thinking.

"He was spouting so many lies, one after another, they were getting all jumbled up and I think he gave me a half dozen excuses for the way he behaved, with each contradicting the other. I'd have laughed, had I not been so upset," she said.

Simon growled, "There's no excuse for what he's done. None at all." He realized his reaction might have come on too strongly, but when he glanced at Mary, she was nodding.

"I told him that," Mary said. She hesitated then, and Simon felt a surge of fear go through him.

"I sense I'm not going to like what he said next," he said quietly.

Her face flickered with something akin to disbelief, before she shook her head slowly. "He asked me to marry him."

Though he knew this was going to happen, Simon still felt his chest tighten. His ears were ringing, and he could see her lips moving, sense Mary was speaking something, but through his terror, all he could wonder was what if she'd said yes?

What would happen to him?

Chapter 19

Mary kept talking, twisting Simon's handkerchief around and around in her fingers, when she looked over at him, and saw such a shocked expression on his face, it nearly made her laugh.

"Wait," Simon said, holding up his hand. "I'm sorry. He...he's asked you to marry him."

"Yes. He said he made a mistake, that he wanted me. Loved me. Apologized so many times. Talking about how he had no meaning in his life now, without me." She shook her head. "I'm sure he wasn't thinking about me at all, but my money. Half the time, he couldn't take his eyes off my handbag."

"So then, what did you say?" Simon asked.

She looked at him in surprise. What had he thought she'd say? "I told him the time had passed. That I had no interest in marrying him, that I have a whole life ahead of me, and he's not in it."

Had his shoulders relaxed just a little? She wondered why. Had he been concerned she'd say yes? Leave?

She couldn't leave. Not at all. The moment Cal had suggested they marry, she realized that it was more than that she no longer loved Cal and wouldn't stand for being treated the way he had treated her. She'd found something else, someone else. There was Julia to care for, and...Simon. Though he wasn't interested in her, she didn't care. She'd stay, take care of Julia, let herself watch him from afar.

Mary couldn't explain it, why she just felt better when Simon was around, but she did. In the sitting room, at the dining table, walking into town, it all felt comfortable and calm.

She didn't want to leave them. And, it didn't appear there was a need to. If he was willing to keep her on as governess, she'd do as before, when she'd lived in service for the Miles family. Work during the day, save her money, and in her free time, work on dresses for children and their dolls. Why, Julia would be wearing them and chances were, eventually, others would want them as well.

If she saved enough, by the time Julia was grown and no longer needed her, the town would be grown too. She could either open her shop or else move somewhere else and do it. As for Simon...well, there was always still just a bit of hope that he'd be ready to have another wife. Perhaps it would be her.

Mary drew in a deep breath as she looked around her. "I'd like to say that's the last I'll see of that man, but I've the feeling it's not."

"I left a message for the sheriff, actually," Simon said. "I asked if he'd stop by this evening. I want to make him aware of the situation, if you don't mind."

"That's a good idea," Mary agreed. "Thank you."

"If I might also add, I think that you made the right choice," Simon said, though he didn't look at her.

"Turning him down? It wasn't much of a choice to begin with," Mary said.

"But you still could have said yes. Thought about the man you'd known and came out for. Hoped to have the things you'd dreamed of."

She nodded. "That's true. But sometimes things don't turn out as you dream. I'd go so far as to say they rarely do. Often, they aren't nearly so wonderful."

"Sometimes they are better," Simon said.

She gave a wry laugh. "That's not been my experience, so, if you say so."

"Still, I'm glad because you deserve a man who loves you, will take care of you, not cast you aside and make you second best, think you'll come at his beck and call."

His words caused that ache in her, and Mary looked down in her lap, hoping that she wouldn't tear up. She wanted those things, wanted that in a man, but wasn't sure she'd get it.

They sat for what felt too long in silence, and she rose to her feet. "Well," she sighed, "wishing and sitting around won't make anything good happen. Perhaps we should go."

Simon stood and picked up the baskets. He gave her a sidelong glance, and said, "I meant every word."

"I appreciate it," Mary said with a small smile. "Maybe I'll be fortunate enough one day to actually meet such a man."

"Maybe you already have," Simon said. Then he stammered, "Just the time isn't right."

"Maybe," Mary said, though she felt doubtful.

No more was said, and they walked in a slightly uncomfortable silence back to the house. Mary couldn't help but keep looking over her shoulder to see if Cal was watching her. Simon began to do the same.

"I'm sorry," Mary said, sheepishly. "I'm just not sure what he's going to do!"

"Which is why I'm going to speak with the sheriff," Simon said. "Do you feel comfortable talking to him as well?"

"I do," Mary said. "I never thought I'd have to do such a thing, and I doubt much will come of it, but at least alerting the sheriff will make me feel better."

"Me as well," Simon said.

They walked into the house's yard, and to the side kitchen door. "Do you know where these things go?" Simon asked, looking at the laden baskets.

"Yes, I believe so," Mary said. "I'll ask Mrs. Thomas if I don't."

"Wonderful," he said, rummaging through to find the tea and the horehound candy. "I don't know where she keeps anything."

Mary unpacked the baskets, putting the items away where she'd noticed them. Soon, all she had left were the ingredients for dinner, and thought perhaps she'd get that started.

Mrs. Thomas had suggested a simple meal, some fried ham and potatoes, green peas, cornbread, and cookies. That would be very easy for her to make.

She bustled about in the kitchen, and was surprised a few moments later when the housekeeper entered.

"Shouldn't you be sitting?" Mary scolded.

"I'll sit right now," Mrs. Thomas promised. "But, it might sound silly, I was a little lonely. I've gotten so used to you being around here, and chatting with you around mealtime preparation, I was missing it."

"Then chat we will," Mary promised. "I've not told you yet what happened when we went to the store."

As she diced potatoes, she told Mrs. Thomas about Cal, and then laughed as the older woman made some snide comments. When had it happened that Mrs. Thomas had become every bit a friend as any other she'd ever had? She appreciated the woman's suggestions and advice, and this was no different.

"Just pay him no mind at all," Mrs. Thomas said. "You are in the right. I'm glad Mr. Alexander wants the sheriff to be aware. That was good thinking on his part."

"I agree," Mary said, stirring the peas. She turned the ham slices in the large skillet. "I'm grateful to him."

"It's none of my business," Mrs. Thomas started, "but do you know what I think?"

"What?" Mary asked, bending over to check the cornbread.

"I think you two are well suited. It's my hope that you become Mrs. Alexander."

Mary stood up so fast, she felt her head spin. Her eyes were wide as she looked at the housekeeper, and she was sure her jaw had dropped. The other woman chuckled. "Admit it," she said. "You are fond of him."

Mary glanced around anxiously, hoping Simon hadn't overheard her, then she whispered, "Yes, but..."

"But what? What excuses are you telling yourself?" the other woman asked bluntly.

She had no answer, but the pink stain she could feel from her embarrassment on her cheeks likely gave away just what she was thinking. That she did like Simon. That she did hope perhaps one day to be Mrs. Alexander.

"Do you know," Mary said suddenly, "when I first got here, I felt so lost and so alone. Though the initial meeting of Simon was quite stressful, I want to thank you. You've taken me under your wing, treated me wonderfully, and I find myself very grateful for your friendship."

Mrs. Thomas beamed at her. "I'm glad to have you here. I hope you'll never leave."

"I'd like that," Mary admitted.

"Like what?" Simon asked, pushing his way through the kitchen door.

"Women's talk," Mrs. Thomas said, "but while you are here, make yourself helpful and put these dishes on the table."

"Yes, ma'am," Simon said, grabbing the bowl of peas in one hand and the pan of cornbread in the other.

Mary gave a soft laugh, while Mrs. Thomas winked at her. A short time later, they were passing the dishes and eating the hearty meal. Mary couldn't help but notice the contentment, how relaxed they all seemed. It was a far cry from that first day's breakfast and dinner, when she'd felt like a stranger. Now, she felt as though she belonged here.

Just as they finished eating, there was a knock at the door. Simon glanced through the window. "Oh! He's here."

"Who is here, Papa?" Julia asked.

"The sheriff. I need to discuss a few things with him. Can I count on you to stay with Mrs. Thomas, in case she has need of anything?" Simon asked.

"We'll go into the sitting room," Julia promised. "I'll read to her from my book."

"That sounds just fine," Mrs. Thomas said, accepting Simon's hand and limping to the sitting room.

Mary quickly smoothed her hair, and then turned as Simon said, "Mary, this is Sheriff Murphy. I thought we'd go into my study, and I can let him know what's been going on."

"Yes, of course," Mary said. "Would you like me to bring in some coffee?"

"I'd sure be appreciative," the sheriff said.

"I'll have it ready in just a moment," Mary promised, turning toward the kitchen.

Luckily, she'd already had water in the kettle warming, and it didn't take long to make a tray. When she walked into Simon's study a few moments later and set the tray down, Simon was briefly explaining his encounter at the bank previously with Cal.

"And this young woman here," Simon explained, "was his former intended."

"That's right," Mary said. She tried to keep her hands from shaking and the shame from her face as she explained what had happened when she arrived, and then again in the general store.

"And at no time, did you ever write to Mr. Lynch, and tell him that the money you had would belong to him?"

"No," Mary said, shaking her head. "I told him I was working, and saving for our life together, for the things we'd need in our home and around our homestead. Each time, I said *we* or *our*. I never told Cal that it was his money, no matter what." She frowned then. "I honestly can't believe he'd even think such a thing."

"Nor can I," Simon said, "but he thought so."

"There's all kinds of folks in the world," Sheriff Murphy said. "Some more honest than others. Now, I can't say as I'm familiar with the man. Can you describe him? Or, better yet, do you have a photograph?"

"I do!" Mary said. "It's in my room. If you'll excuse me, I'll fetch it for you."

Mary hurried from the room and up the stairs. While the sheriff hadn't said that he'd be able to do anything to help her, just another person knowing what had happened, and that Cal was trying to get something not rightly his, made her feel better.

She just wished she could stop telling the part about him with the other woman. What must others think of her?

She walked down the hallway, and started to twist the knob on the door. Something made her stop then. An instinct, a warning deep in her stomach. Mary pressed her ear close. Inside of her room, she could hear someone moving around. Things being rifled through.

She pressed her lips together, and pushed open the door. "Julia Alexander," she started, "just what do you—"

But it wasn't Julia in her room.

Cal stood there, digging through her trunk.

Mary backed up, but as Cal came closer toward her, an angry look on his face, she did the only thing that she could think of that might save her.

With all of her might, she pushed at the heavy side table in the hallway, hoping to barricade the door, and screamed. A hand wrapped around her mouth, another one pulling her arm sharply behind her back.

Chapter 20

"I'm very concerned," Simon said. "There was something in his face, his eyes, that I just didn't like."

"I'm glad you let me know," the sheriff said. "His name sounds familiar...Lynch. Lynch." The sheriff narrowed his eyes, looking off into the distance. "It'll come to me, but seems to me, about six, seven months ago, another fellow came to me with a complaint about him. Asking if something was legal."

"Is that so?" Simon asked. "I know he's a gambler. At least, that's what I hear, both from him and from Mrs. Thomas."

"That's it!" the sheriff said suddenly. "The man who came to me lost his—"

A sudden shrill scream from upstairs sounded before it was abruptly cut off. Simon wasted no time. He rushed from his study, the sheriff right on his heels. From the sitting room, he could hear Julia calling his name. "Stay there," he ordered loudly, sure Mrs. Thomas would keep her there.

When Simon got to the top of the stairs, he froze. He couldn't see Mary, but he knew the scream had been hers. Just...where was she?

"Which room is hers?" the sheriff asked.

"This one," Simon said, indicating the closed door.

He tried the knob, but it was locked. "Mary? Mary!"

There was a crash inside the room, and Simon hit the door with his shoulder.

"Do you have a key?" the sheriff asked.

"Yes!" Simon ran for it. He kept a set of keys in his bedroom. He pulled open the drawer he kept them in, fishing around. In frustration, he dumped the entire contents out, and then lunged as soon as he saw the keyring. Hurriedly, Simon returned, shoving the one for Mary's room into the lock. The key twisted, the door opened, and he was furious, and quite alarmed, to see Cal Lynch standing there, trying to push Mary out the second-floor window.

"Stop right there," the sheriff said from his spot next to Simon.

"Let her go," Simon said, unable to take his eyes off of the terrible sight in front of him. Mary was partially out the window. If Cal gave her enough of a push from behind, she was sure to fall.

Cal's eyes darted between him and the sheriff. "You give me the money, I'll let her go," he finally said. "It's mine. I only want what's mine."

"I can't talk to you with Mary hanging out the window," Simon said as calmly as he could. "Bring her back in. Then I'll talk, and you can tell me about this money you want."

Cal hesitated, but only for a moment, as his desire to have the money outweighed his need to harm Mary. He yanked her in, and she slid down to the floor, her back against the wall and relief on her face.

"Let's talk!" Cal said. He frowned, seeming to notice the sheriff. "Who are you?"

"This is Sheriff Murphy," Simon said. "So if I were you, I'd not cause any trouble."

Cal snorted. "Cal Lynch has never been afraid of any sheriff."

"Lynch!" the sheriff suddenly said. "I remember now. He doesn't own that homestead of his. Won it in a game of cards, and took it illegally."

"But the land office had him listed," Simon said, confused.

"Likely because Cal here went and told them it was his, and that he'd gotten it from the other man, Jacobson. Nope, it's not his. I'm not even sure he's got one."

"Why start from scratch when you can take one partway done?" Cal asked with a shrug. "What's it matter? It's mine. Won it fair and square and my name is in the land office."

"The law don't agree with that," Sheriff Murphy said. "Got to live on it five years once you claim it. That's not you who has been on it for the time you've claimed."

"Is that true, Cal?" Mary asked, her voice trembling. "That was another lie you told me? You didn't even go and get land for us?"

"What does it matter? Do you know how hard it is to find a good claim? All the work involved? This way was much easier. Woulda still been ours," Cal said.

"But it's not right! It wasn't yours! I could have married you, and we'd have been pushed off when the truth came out. Homeless," she whispered.

Simon felt badly for her. She already knew Cal wasn't the kind of man he'd pretended to be, and now more was revealed.

"You are under arrest, Cal Lynch," the sheriff said.

"What for?" Cal asked.

"Assault, for one," Sheriff Murphy said. "I saw you trying to push her out the window. I bet we look, she'll have some bruises on her. That's battery. Next, we've got unpaid loans, stealing land. Why I bet if I keep on digging, I'll learn all kinds of things. Get you put away a real long time. But not here. Nope, violating a law like you've done with the Homestead Act gets you sent to a bigger place. Harsher."

"You're lying," Cal snarled.

"Maybe, maybe not. Now, you gonna come quiet?" Sheriff Murphy asked.

Cal turned his glare to Simon. "What's this to you? Why didn't you just give me the loan? I wasn't hurting anybody. I'd have just taken the money and gone."

"Like you're trying to do now?" Simon asked.

"Yes. That's right," Cal said. "Look, you've got my word. A few hundred, and I'm gone. Heck, I'll leave town. Won't ever return. Mary," he said, looking at her, "I'll leave you be. Really. I wasn't trying to hurt you. Just scare you a little. Get what was mine. What you'd promised."

"That money was for us," Mary said. "Us. Our future."

"Well, let's have it," Cal said. "You can still marry me. Let's go, right now! There's still time, and you can make me a late supper."

"I'd never spend my days with a man like you," Mary said, her voice cold. She deliberately turned her head away.

"Fine. Banker. How about it?" Cal asked. "Where's my money?"

"A man like you isn't ever satisfied with anything," Simon said. "I've seen it dozens of times over. It doesn't matter what you have. What you get, are given. It's just never enough to make you happy."

"Why does it matter to you?" Cal asked. "Not your money. It's the bank's money. Mary's money. What's any of that got to do with you? Why do you care?"

As soon as the words escaped Cal's lips, a strange tension filled the room. Simon knew this was the time he could give an answer, any answer, or none at all.

Or, he could tell the truth. The truth about how he cared for Mary. Didn't want to see her hurt. Had developed feelings for her.

But there was a roomful of people. It didn't seem the best time.

But was there ever a good time for such a thing? And what about how Mary might feel?

Simon could feel the weight of three sets of eyes looking at him. He weighed his options carefully. And then, he decided.

"Why it matters?" Simon started. He could still feel the eyes staring at him, Mary's, Cal's, the sheriff's. But it didn't matter. He wasn't going to hide his feelings any longer. "I'll tell you why."

Chapter 21

Simon was aware that everyone's full attention was on him. It felt like his mouth should have dried up, but instead, it kept talking. Giving this sort of confession in a room full of near strangers—like the sheriff and Cal—wasn't something he thought he'd do, ever, but he'd seen how hurt Mary had looked when she talked about Cal.

He couldn't even imagine how she felt right now, with her former intended trying to push her out the window, threatening her for money.

His eyes sought Mary's, and he said, "Because, even though it doesn't make sense, even though I've not known Mary for long, I know there's something special about her. I know that each moment she's around me, I feel happier. My daughter feels happier. The things that were missing in our lives, that we didn't even know were missing, are complete when Mary is around."

The words poured from him, and Simon realized that he'd never felt so right in anything he'd ever said. He kept going. "Mary, I was angry at first when you came, because it forced me to confront the pain I'd been wrestling with since Meghan died. The worry and feeling of being alone, that I couldn't ever be happy again. But then, you changed me."

"Blah, blah, this is all great," Cal said, "but I can't wait around all day. What's any of this got to do with me?"

Simon ignored the man, his attention focused fully on Mary, whose beautiful face was filled with surprise. "I think Meghan must have known she was going to leave me. The day before she did, she told me that she wanted me to live, and to be happy. That it was important to keep my heart open. How it wasn't selfish." Simon swallowed hard. "When we were in the attic, and Julia had shown you her mother's things, and we spoke, you and I, I realized then that I wasn't living. I wasn't happy. And, I was being selfish."

"You weren't," Mary said quickly. She stood and started to step toward him, but Cal pulled her back.

"Not so fast," Cal growled.

Just as he had, Mary ignored the man. "You were trying to keep yourself and Julia from pain. It's not a crime to want to spare yourself suffering. You are human, after all."

"But now, I have a new kind of pain," Simon said. "I've grown very fond of you. More than fond. I can't stop thinking of you. And I'm not going to be a fool, like Cal was, and miss an opportunity if you will have me."

"Now see here," Cal interrupted. "I'm not a fool. I know how great Mary is. Mary," he said, turning to her, "I think we had a rough patch, that's all. But—"

"But nothing," Mary said. "You've embarrassed me, threatened me, played me false. I did nothing but work my fingers to the bone, long days and spare moments on the side, to save for our future. I was true to you, but I refuse to ever again believe a word that you say. If you'd loved me, if you'd cared for me at all, you'd have never treated me the way that you did."

Simon couldn't help but feel a little bit pleased at how Cal's face fell, and his lower lip pushed out, like a petulant child. "You've heard the lady," Simon said, "and the sheriff is here. It's time you leave. In his custody."

Cal lunged for the window, but the sheriff was quicker, and grabbed him by his collar and hauled him out of Mary's room. Simon followed, then paused, "If you need to take a few moments to yourself, I understand. I'm going to help the sheriff get Cal back to town."

"I think...I think," Mary said, taking a deep breath, "I'll go and check on Mrs. Thomas and Julia."

He nodded, and started toward the stairs. "Wait!" Mary's soft voice called out. "Did you...did you mean those things? Or were they simply for Cal's benefit?"

Simon hurried over to her, taking her hands in his. "Oh, Mary, I meant those and so much more," he whispered, leaning close and grazing his cheek against hers. "When I get back, can we finish that conversation? But without such a large audience? There's more I want to say."

"I'd like that," Mary said, her cheeks turning pink.

He brushed his thumb over one, and then smiled at her, before hurrying away down the stairs, where the sheriff was pushing Cal out of the front door.

"I'll walk with you," Simon said.

"Appreciate it, Mr. Alexander," Sheriff Murphy said. "Don't want this one getting away."

"I was framed!" Cal howled. "It's all a lie! Everyone's against me!"

"Hush," the sheriff said, then looked at Simon. "So what do you think about all this rain?"

They talked over Cal's protests as they marched him back to town, and the sheriff's office.

"I'll get my deputy to sit a spell with him," the sheriff said. "I'll also be sure to let you know what the outcome is. The circuit judge will be riding through pretty soon. Bet he'll know just what to do."

"I appreciate it," Simon said. "Mary will too, I'm sure. Have a good evening."

He left and hurried back to the house. Simon just hoped when he did get back, that Mary would still be open to hearing the things he'd been longing to tell her.

He stepped onto his porch, and hesitated. His eyes swept over the mountains in the distance, the purples and blues rising up to meet the sky. He loved it here, but he loved Mary more. If she wanted to leave, he'd go wherever she wanted. As long as she wanted him.

Would she? He hoped so. All he had left to do was ask. Swallowing hard, he pushed open the front door. Why was he so nervous? All he had to do was say, Mary, I love you. Will you consider being my wife? Part of my future? Not hard at all.

But then he caught sight of her, a tray in her hands as she set it on a side table and offered Mrs. Thomas some tea. Their eyes met, and every single word he'd wanted to say fled his mind.

Mary held her hands before her. "You're back," she said.

"Yes," Simon said. He glanced at Mrs. Thomas.

"She told me everything," the housekeeper said. And then she winked. "Why don't you two finish your conversation while Julia and I have some cookies in the kitchen?"

Mrs. Thomas stood, and left with Julia, who grinned and winked several times very obviously at him, and before he knew it, he was standing there, alone with Mary, his heart pounding so heavily, he thought it might burst through his chest.

Chapter 22

Mary's eyes followed Mrs. Thomas and Julia. Right after Simon and the sheriff had left, pulling an unwilling Cal who'd said a few words she hoped Julia would forget, Mary had explained, some parts in whispers, to Mrs. Thomas what had happened, including nearly being pushed out the window.

Mrs. Thomas had demanded she tell her if she had any aches and pains later, and insisted she'd give her as much horehound candy as she needed—and hobble to the store herself for more if needed. The fierce tone had nearly brought Mary to tears. She felt so grateful for the other woman's companionship.

Now that Simon had returned, and it was just the two of them, Mary wasn't sure what to do. She felt quite nervous.

What if he'd had time to change his mind on his way back to her?

"Mary," Simon said, clearing his throat, "I..."

She waited. He seemed a little nervous too, but she wasn't sure in what way. In the, I love you way, or the I'm not interested in you way. Mary wished he'd hurry and speak, but she made herself be patient.

A look Mary knew was Simon organizing his thoughts washed over his face, and after a second, he nodded. "Right. I'm not the best at this. Quite out of practice, really. So, if I say it wrong, you'll forgive me, I hope?"

"Maybe," she teased. "Maybe I won't."

He laughed at that, and the sound made her feel better.

"Mary, I'd like to spend the rest of my days with you," he said. "For you to be my wife, to be Julia's mother, and to be a part of our family."

She wanted that too. But...

Mary took a deep breath. "Are you sure? I mean, are you ready for that? I'm never going to try and replace Meghan. But, I do want some of your love." She was ashamed, as tears sprang to her eyes. Did that sound desperate? Needy?

"My sweet Mary," Simon said, drawing close to her. "You will have my love. There's room in my heart for you, and for Julia, and for Meghan. There's room as well for any other children who come along."

Mary searched his eyes and saw the truth. "I'm glad. I want to honor her memory, and her gift of Julia. I want to be sure you understand I'd never take that away."

Gently, Simon ran his thumb across her cheek. "You are wonderful, do you know that? I will always love Meghan, because she was my first love and the mother of my beautiful daughter. But I will also always love you, because you have brought me out of my darkness, filled me with light and happiness again. You awoke me from the numbness. Your love isn't replacing anyone. It's adding to it. I hope that makes sense."

Mary leaned her head against his chest. "It does." She looked up at him, "I would be so happy to be your wife, Simon."

"I want you to be more than that, if you want," Simon said.

"What do you mean?" Mary asked.

"I mean the dresses you make," Simon said, and then walked over to the tiny doll dress Mary had been working on that evening. "I know you've also thought about having your own business. If that's something you want as well, I want you to have it. And if you think it's not something you can do in this town, then we can move somewhere else. Since I manage several banks, we have many options. There are larger cities. Whatever will make you happy."

That wasn't what she'd expected to hear. Mary had never thought that her husband—whoever he would be—would offer such a thing. It rendered her speechless. For a long moment, all she could do was blink and look at him.

Finally, her mind started to work again. "That is very generous of you," she said. "I will think on it."

"Take all the time you want. My offer will stand."

"Simon, I couldn't ask for a more understanding, and kind, and generous person than you are being to me," Mary said. "I know we had an unusual start, but I don't think I'd change it for anything."

"Neither would I," Simon said, and he leaned in so close, Mary could feel his breath on her face. She tipped her head up slightly, and—

A sudden crash startled Mary and Simon. They looked over to see a sheepish Julia standing there at the doorway.

"I'm sorry," she said. "I dropped my book. Am I in time?"

"In time for what?" Mary asked.

"To hear if you are going to be my other mother," Julia said eagerly. "Is she, Papa?"

"Why, yes, yes she is," Simon said, holding out one of his arms.

Julia ran into their embrace, and Mary squeezed her tightly.

"I'm so happy," Simon said. "I wasn't sure I'd ever be again, but I know, right now, I have all I want, and all I could ever need."

"I love you, Simon," Mary said softly.

"I love you, Mary." And then he finished the kiss, and Mary thought she was floating away in happiness.

Epilogue

One year later

Mary rested on the sofa in the sitting room, sewing a doll's dress. One day, she'd taken Julia inside the general store, and she'd been carrying her doll. Once they'd learned Mary had made the doll's dress, the shop owners begged her to consider making doll dresses for them to sell. To her surprise, they absolutely flew off the shelves, and several a week sold. Julia began to help her soon after, so that she could also earn a little extra pocket money while improving her sewing skills. Perhaps one day, Mary thought, she'd advertise that she could make matching dresses for little girls and their dolls, and see if the store wanted them as well.

She let out a small yawn and put the dress down, fondly watching Julia on the floor with the baby, and remembering what had happened just two weeks before.

"When the baby comes, what should we call it?" Julia asked, gently resting her hand on Mary's stomach.

"Nothing seems quite right," Mary murmured. "I think I'm running out of names. Alyssa. Iris? Poppy? What about Louise or Mathilda?"

"I like Grace," Simon said. "Carissa?"

"Leah!" Mrs. Thomas said. "Or Millie? Rosalee?"

"That one is pretty," Mary said, "but it doesn't feel right."

"Charlotte?" Simon suggested.

"Caroline!" Mrs. Thomas countered. "Elizabeth."

"It could be a boy," Simon said. "Asher. Eli? Maybe Andrew."

"I've always been partial to Billy or Gavin or Kody," Mrs. Thomas said eagerly.

"Mama, what about this?" Julia asked, and pointed to a sentence in her book.

"Cordelia," Mary read. "This name has multiple meanings, including "heart," "daughter of the sea," and "jewel of the sea."

"A sea is like an ocean," Julia explained. "Like our hearts are. Big enough for everyone."

"I think that's the perfect name if it's a little girl," Mary said, smiling at Julia. "What do you think?" she asked Simon and Mrs. Thomas.

Mrs. Thomas was dabbing at tears, while Simon was clearing his throat. "I think that's a wonderful name," he said with a nod.

And a few weeks later, it had been the perfect name. Now, she was watching as Julia held a picture of her mother, and was telling Cordelia all about her, and how one day, she'd show her the treasures in the attic.

"Thank you," Simon said, as he looked over at her. "For letting her include Meghan."

"She's as much a part of our story as you or I," Mary said. "Without her, we wouldn't be here together."

"It's true," Simon agreed.

Mary's eyes took in the scene before her. Julia, happily talking to her sister, Simon reading a book, and Mrs. Thomas, sipping on tea while she knitted.

She'd never tell Cal, but she almost owed him a thank you.

Almost.

After the circuit judge had come through, he'd made Cal give the homestead back to the rightful claimants. He'd also demanded Cal pay back his debts, declared that Mary owed him nothing, and told him to leave town.

She'd not seen him since the hearing.

"What are you thinking about?" Simon asked.

"Cal," she told him.

Simon frowned.

"And how glad I am now that he did what he did," she explained.

"I'm not glad for the pain you went through, but I'm glad too," Simon said.

When she'd set out for Oregon just over a year before, this hadn't been her westward dream. Yet, life had turned out so much better than she'd imagined. All she'd ever longed for was right in front of her. Home.

Want more?

If you enjoyed this story, you might also enjoy these.

A Journey for Leah

A victim of misplaced affections, Leah Dearing dreams of starting over in Oregon where she can own land and put her past behind her. But as a single woman, she is refused a place in the wagon train, no matter that she's more than capable of doing all she needs. Desperate to build a new life for herself, she is willing to do anything—including a marriage in name only.

Stanley Keith has no intention of heading out West with a bride until he overhears Leah's plight. He knows the way will be difficult and many don't make it. To top it off, he's got a woman waiting for him when he gets there. Yet, something about her determination sparks in him, and before he's realized it he offers to let her join him on his journey in exchange for her cooking and companionship.

However, the trail is long and dangerous, and the challenges they face might be more than either realized. Especially when one of them starts to fall in love...and the reminder of another waiting for them at the end of the trail becomes impossible to ignore.

***

Alyssa's Desperate Plan
"Yer too small on the top. I want a bigger woman."
Alyssa Moore never expected *that* to be the reason her prospective groom turned her away after one look. Now, with almost no money and no family to turn to for help, she's stuck waiting in a small town until the mail-order bride agency that sent her finds another match. She's embarrassed to seek help because that isn't her only mortifying situation, but it's all she can do.
When an upset woman finds him to ask for help posting a letter, Peter West is more than curious about her. As he learns more, he wonders...what would happen if her letter didn't post? At least for a few days. Would she consider staying there, with someone like him? He knows

it's pointless. A beautiful woman like that wouldn't want a man like him.

As Alyssa becomes desperate and Peter tries to summon his courage, they'll each discover there's far more to a person than meets the eye—and that friendship and love can blossom in the most unexpected of ways.

https://www.amazon.com/Alyssas-Desperate-Rejected-Mail-Order-Brides-ebook/dp/B0CN8FKZX7

Note from Author

Thank you for taking the time to read *Westward Dreams*. Could I ask for one small favor? Reviews like yours on Amazon mean so much to me and help others to find my books! Even just a single line means a lot!

Also...

Want a FREE book?

Stop by my website to get your no strings attached **FREE book**. It's my gift to you, as a thank you for reading this one.

www.sarahlambbooks.com

About the Author

Sarah writes captivating characters and clean romance that's anything BUT boring! From heartbreaking moments to heartwarming tales, get swept away in either historical or small town romance that pulls you in until the last page.

Nestled in the Blue Ridge Mountains of Virginia where she's married to her Texan husband, you'll find Sarah creating her next book, homeschooling her two boys, or volunteering in her community.

Want more of Sarah's books? Find them all on Amazon!

https://www.amazon.com/stores/Sarah-Lamb/author/B098H3SGLK